Chicago Haunts 3

LOCKED UP STORIES FROM AN OCTOBER CITY

Chicago Haunts 3

LOCKED UP STORIES FROM AN OCTOBER CITY

by Ursula Bielski

Thunder Bay Press

Holt, Michigan 48842

Chicago Haunts 3
by Ursula Bielski

Published August 2009
Thunder Bay Press
Holt, MI 48842

ISBN: 978-1-933272-15-3

First Edition

13   12   11   10   09   1   2   3   4   5

Cover photograph by the author.
Book and cover design by Julie Taylor.

Printed in the United States of America
by McNaughton & Gunn, Inc.
Saline, MI USA
August 2009

To "Chicago Ed," the late Eddie Schwartz, &
Richard T. Crowe, the city's original ghost hunter,
Thank you for keeping us awake.

(T)he past experience revived in the meaning
Is not the experience of one life only
But of many generations—not forgetting
Something that is probably quite ineffable:
The backward look behind the assurance
Of recorded history, the backward half-look
Over the shoulder, towards the primitive terror.

... (T)he moments of agony... are likewise permanent
With such permanence as time has. We appreciate this better
In the agony of others, nearly experienced...

But the torment of others remains an experience
Unqualified, unworn by subsequent attrition.
People change, and smile: but the agony abides.
Time the destroyer is time the preserver...

—T.S. Eliot
Four Quartets: The Dry Salvages

CONTENTS

PREFACE

The book you are about to read is a book of true events that have deeply affected the history of Chicago and its people, and of the sometimes incredible phenomena that have been perceived after these events. The stories are ones that I began collecting after the publication of *Chicago Haunts* (1997) and *More Chicago Haunts* (2000), and which I have investigated and researched since the founding of Chicago Hauntings, Inc., an organization which provides lectures and tours illuminating "what lies beneath" the often whitewashed history of the city, and which investigates—in a very real way—the still unexplained phenomena often associated with this history.

I know that many young people have enjoyed my previous books; indeed I have been honored and moved by the numerous claims of those who "began to love reading" after they picked up one of my books in the school library—or had one pressed on them by an earnest librarian. I want to warn readers that this volume is a good deal more graphic than the former two, a quality resulting not from a desire for a more sensationalized or edgy book, but from a desire to tell the stories straight, perhaps to help explain why so much unrest remains.

There are accounts in this book of the deeds of men like Richard Speck and John Wayne Gacy, some of the most diabolical murderers the world has known. There are stories about the tragic past of the Dunning property, where thousands were institutionalized, neglected and, eventually, buried in the potter's field just recently discovered there. And there are the disturbing retellings of the events of recent years: the Brown's Chicken Massacre, the school bus accident at Fox River Grove, the porch collapse of 2003 that led to more than a dozen deaths, and the terrible night of the E2 nightclub stampede.

As I wrote this book, I woke from most nights plagued by nightmares. Readers may have them, too, or may be tougher than I in digesting these atrocities—and the attendant phenomena reported in this volume. I hope that all come away, however, haunted by Chicago's very real past—if not its literal ghosts--and unwilling to forget those who have been so permanently affected by the events and people who have shaped it, for better or worse.

ACKNOWLEDGMENTS

Many people over many years helped with this book, whether they knew it or not. Information, stories, leads came from so many anonymous readers, tour guests, lecture attendees, and others. I wish I knew all of their names to thank them. These are the ones who I came to know because of their kind responses to my requests for help, or because they approached me with experiences and ideas, or because they were willing to connect themselves to these sometimes controversial phenomena: Thomas Gokey, Michael Fassbender, Tom Tunney, Daniel Pogorzelski, John Maloof, Michael Quinlan, Jennifer LaCivita, Johnny D., Nicole Carter, Meagan Drnek, John Bell, Edward Shanahan, John Suerth, Kathy Doore, Patricia Turnage, and Thomas Stahler.

I would have had few facts to back up many of these reports if not for the wealth of information provided by the *Chicago Tribune,* the Chicago Public Library, the Forest Preserve Districts of Cook and Lake Counties, the Chicago History Museum, the Jefferson Park Historical Society, the Art Institute of Chicago, the Newberry Library and, of course, those at all of the establishments about which I've written: the Congress Plaza, the Sheffield House, Ann Sather's, Mrs. Murphy and Sons Irish Bistro, Odin Tatu, the 12-Step House, the Hancock Center, the Edgewater Apartments, the Cook County Courthouse, Macy's, the Oriental Theater, the Museum of Science and Industry, and all the others.

I especially want to thank my brother, Adalbert Bielski, who knows where everything is and when everything happened, even when no one else remembers. Often, when I had no clue about a location or event, the information was at the tip of his tongue in seconds flat.

I'm grateful for the tolerance of my photography at some of the very sensitive sites in this book, including the Dunning property, the former Gacy property on Summerdale Avenue, the Pinecrest Apartments, the Jeffrey Manor Townhouse where the Speck murders occurred, the site of the 2003 porch collapse, and the building which housed the former Epitome/E2 nightclub. I hope that residents will understand the need for such photos, and in capturing the images of these sites I hoped to satisfy the natural curiosity of readers for such visuals without unnecessary and potentially disruptive pilgrimages.

I am extremely grateful for the beautiful photographs pro-vided by Michael Spudic, who walked many miles to capture his images for me, Christine Zenino, whose loving photographs of the Dunning property provided literal and emotional snapshots of a reality that no longer exists, and Angela Larson, whose truly haunting images seem infused with a miraculous life; they en-tranced me from the first shot. I'm so grateful that these artistic and insightful souls were willing to share their own spirits—and time and diligence—with this project.

So much support, encouragement and inspiration has come from so many people in the world of ghost research but especially Jeff Belanger, Mark Macy, Jeff Rezman, Ed Shanahan, and Wanda and Mike Spudic. Thank you for making me keep thinking about these phenomena.

In the preparation of the manuscript I am deeply indebted to Elizabeth Rintoul, who was invaluable in fleshing out the tedious accounts of the Speck and Gacy murders and the suicide of Frank Nitti, as well as the story of Manteno State Hospital. Don Panarese sweetly read the chapters I left at his door each morning and gave me sound advice, not only about the writing but also about some of the sensitive content that concerned me. Sharon Woodhouse of Lake Claremont Press, the original publisher of the *Chicago Haunts* books, generously offered to read the manuscript from a Chicagoan's point of view to assure accuracy to my new Michigan-based publishing house, Thunder Bay Press, and David was always ready to patch holes in my thinking so that the finished product made "Chicago sense." At Thunder Bay, both editor Julie Taylor and publisher Sam Speigel made me feel like one of the family from the start. Thank you.

Finally, as always, I can't thank those closest enough. In particular, I am most indebted to my mom, who was always there to watch my daughters so I could go digging—whether through real rubble or clippings files, and the wonderful Accove kids—Julie, Tony, and Susie—who were always happy to distract my daughters for a few hours so their mother could work.

I thank, so much, those two little girls who tried not to fight too much while their mom was working around the clock at the end, even through the nicest days of summer, and Don, who ordered me constantly to "get to work" or "get some sleep."

Introduction

My Own True Ghost Story

The dead say nothing
And the dead know much
And the dead hold
Under their tongues
A locked-up story.

—Carl Sandburg
Chicago Poems

*M*y paranormal life, with all its awe and impossibility, began with my earliest memory of all: waking up in my little bed sometime after midnight to the sound of ghostly footsteps on the stairs. The phenomenon was one that occurred every single night in the house on Bell Avenue, on Chicago's Northwest Side, from the day my mother and father bought it until the time I began high school some fourteen years later, but it was one to which I would never grow accustomed. In fact, I know now that it was the fear of that nightly visitor that led me to a lifelong interest in the Other Side.

The house on Bell Avenue had been built by my mother's great-uncle, Andrew Erbach, who helped develop the largely German neighborhood of North Center, an enclave of the Lake View settlement of Chicago. My mother grew up two blocks away from our home, and even as a young woman working her way through school at Victor Adding Machine, she'd heard stories of the house's haunting. Years later, my mom became a fifth-grade teacher at St. Benedict Elementary School, just across the street, where I would attend, and there she met my father, Adalbert Bielski, a beat cop on traffic duty who led her across Irving Park Road each morning and afternoon.

When the two married in the fall of 1966, my dad's apartment at Fullerton and Kedvale became their home together, but almost at once, my mom found herself expecting my older brother, Adalbert James, and she longed, naturally, to find a proper house. Her search began and ended at the run-down orange brick home her uncle had built, which at the time stood across from the convent of St. Benedict, the communal residence of many of the school's teachers. When my mom saw the "For Sale" sign on the property, she was enchanted. Nothing would stop her from making this unlikely place her family's home. When my dad saw it, however, he was less than enamored of the ruined floors, the dilapidated plaster, and the second floor bathroom toilet, which had fallen through the ceiling to the frontroom below. "It's a barn," he said. My mother was optimistic.

As the months went by, no offers came, and my mother became a frequent drop-in at the real estate office, asking whether the price of the place had decreased. Though endless weeks went by without a nudge, one day, at last, her persistence paid off. The asking price of $22,000 had dropped to $17,500, and my dad said okay.

**My dad and mom, around the time they bought
the house on Bell Avenue.**

For months, while my mom waited for the baby to arrive, my dad worked to make the house livable. The job went far from smoothly, as he used fly-by-night labor recruited from the Blue-bird Tap at Ashland Avenue and Irving Park Road, but sometime after my brother was born, the first floor had reached a state akin to livable, and the Bielskis moved in.

For two years, my mom and dad slept in the formal dining room on the first floor. My older brother, Adalbert James, slept in a crib in the adjacent kitchen. During those years Chicago cops worked rotating shifts, some months from 8 A.M. to 4 P.M., some from 4 to midnight. Other months, they'd endure the first watch, from midnight until just after dawn. During the nights over the course of those years, when my father was on duty, there were times my mom would awaken in that makeshift bedroom sure she had heard sounds from the uninhabitable upstairs halls. Decades later, she would still recall the breathless times spent standing in the darkened kitchen alone after midnight, my brother softly breathing in his crib, as she strained, listening with every nerve, to verify some movement beyond her imagination. When the upstairs rooms were finally renovated, some three years later, the doubts she'd had about the reality of the sounds instantly dissipated. In fact, in the course of a single night, we all became believers.

I don't quite remember that very first night we slept in the upstairs rooms—my mom and dad at the top of the stairs, my brother and I at the back of the house—but my mom and dad (and even my brother) always would. The night came during my dad's turn on the evening watch, so he returned home soon after midnight and, after my mom had fried him a plate of eggs, they climbed the stairs to bed. Sleep came quickly, but almost at once they were awakened by the sound of footfalls on the ancient oak stairs, the treads creaking in succession from foyer to landing, for all the world as if someone were stealthily making his way to the second floor from the front hall downstairs. Instinctively, my dad reached to the nightstand for his service revolver and, a moment later, swung around the door frame to confront the intruder. To his astonishment there was no one there; though, as he looked down the steps, the sound of the footfalls continued as clearly as before. After a few moments, my anxious mom called out to him. His response was: "Lory, come look at this."

And so, that night, the two stood together at the top of the stairs, mesmerized by what they could hear but neither see nor quite believe. Roused by the sound of voices and the blazing hall lights, my brother and I—just four and three years old—soon joined them. I am told that I stared for the briefest second then at once began to cry.

For thirteen years, the footsteps continued, each and every night, jarring us awake each time as they had that very first time. My brother and I grew up, my mother and father grew older; we—and the house—changed in so many ways. The footfalls

Photograph by the author

**The staircase in my childhood home,
where it all started.**

were a constant for all of us, something strangely familiar and utterly reliable, though the nature of them completely undermined any sense of stability we might have garnered from anything else as habitual.

Along with the footsteps, another movement—at the time totally imperceptible—began that first night, in that house, and deep inside each of us. We couldn't have known it then, but that night a door opened for all of us. That door swung wide on an immoveable sense of wonder and curiosity—and yes, fear—that started with those footfalls and goes on even now. That night, the house put us under a spell that has never quite been broken. And though, thirteen years later, the footsteps finally ended, that door has never closed.

◆

It wasn't until I was nearly thirty and *Chicago Haunts*, my first book, was published that we discovered the likely identity behind those seemingly endless phantom footfalls. We learned the story from Marilyn Gulan, a friend of my mother's who had taught with her at Horace Greeley Elementary School, not far from the lake. Before my parents bought the house on Bell Avenue, Marilyn and her husband had lived in the single frame house directly across the street from our future home. According to Marilyn, our former tenants were an elderly brother and sister who had grown up in the house and, after their parents and other siblings had passed on, remained. The sister suffered a serious mental illness which confined her to the house for her whole life. Most likely, she should have been institutionalized but was not. Day after day, Marilyn told us, she would sit at the window of the house on Bell Avenue, staring out into the wider world that was, since infancy, lost to her.

Heartbreakingly, this woman had longed since girlhood to become a nun—a path, like most others, closed to her because of her health. What she did, then, was to participate in her longed-for vocation the best she knew how. Each morning, she would adorn herself in a long, black dress and a black veil she had sewn herself. This was the garb she wore each day during those hours—and years—of sitting at the front room window.

It's hardly surprising that the house gained a reputation as haunted, with its somber, unmoving woman in black stirring the imaginations of the hundreds of school children tramping past the place each day, terrified and entranced at once by her mystery.

But that the house was *in fact* haunted? That the rumors were more than mere legends? How to explain it? It was a question that has tugged at my mind since that first footfall, because the Woman in Black was not the only entity that haunted me as a girl, nor the only inspiration for my future life of ghost hunting. In fact, one of the most enchanted places I've ever known was just two blocks away, my grandmother's house, where my mother had been born.

The house was a towering Victorian two-flat, quite unlike the typical Chicago two-flat I live in today. Upstairs, my grandma, Frances, and her husband, Joseph, raised six children—three boys and three girls—in a cramped two bedroom apartment. For most of her life, my mother's bed was the front room sofa, where she would study by the light of street lamps before turning in, while her brothers slept in the attic and the baby in the formal dining room. As restricted as the living arrangements were, the house was rendered magical by an astonishing garden at the back of the house, overflowing with heirloom poppies, floxgloves, bleeding hearts, and forget-me-nots. It was made mystical by an aging sundial, a wooden windmill my Uncle Joe had built, and a rock garden and grotto he had fashioned in my grandmother's honor. It would be impossible to describe the impact that garden had on my cousins, my brother, and myself when we were growing up. The eight of us often spent days or weeks together there in the summertime, but I will mention that many of those nights were spent on the back porch of my grandmother's flat overlooking the garden while my aunts and uncles and my older cousins told thrilling stories of the paranormal.

Photograph by the author

**My grandmother's house,
a haven of hauntings and history.**

It was on those summer nights that I first heard of baby Frances, my grandmother's firstborn, who had died of pneumonia as an infant and whose cries even we sometimes heard drifting through the house as we slept on the front room floor during those hot nights. It was on those evenings that I first heard my grandmother's stories of growing up in Wisconsin at a time when embalming was unheard of and loved ones were often buried alive. It was on one of those nights that I first heard the story of my great-great aunt who sat up at her own wake and attacked her husband with the fireplace poker for mistakenly declaring her dead.

Years later, when I was in high school and my grandmother was gone, my Uncle Joe lived alone in her old flat where a heart attack took him, one night, to the other side. While he was alive,

Uncle Joe had spent the first hour of each morning feeding the birds in the backyard. He would tear up a loaf of bread and, sitting at the old wooden table, scatter it over the porch railing for the sparrows, cardinals, and pigeons that would congregate in the garden at dawn. The morning after his death, my Uncle Norbert, who lived downstairs with Aunt Frannie, came out of their flat to take out the garbage. As he passed under the porch to make his way to the alley, Uncle Norb was showered with torn-up bread, as if my uncle were still alive feeding the birds as he had always done.

The events that transpired at my grandmother's house had company, too, at her son Eugene's home a few blocks west. When Eugene married Catherine Schroeder, they moved into a single-family house across Western Avenue in which the previous owner had committed suicide, hanging himself in the garage one winter morning.

Uncle Gene was an insurance salesman and had worked out of the den off the front room of the pleasant home, so he and my aunt were home together most of the time. One night each week, however, Uncle Gene would go out to his lodge meeting leaving Aunt Katie in the house alone. As soon as he closed the front door behind him, as Katie would tell, the locked kitchen door would swing open, almost as if in response. Sure that this was the ghost of the former tenant coming in from the garage, Aunt Katie (utterly fearless) would call out, "Come on in! Gene's gone out!"

◆

When I wrote the first volume of this series, *Chicago Haunts*, I dedicated the book to my father, Adalbert Stanislaus Bielski, and readers have often asked me why. It's no secret to those who know me that I credit much of my interest in the paranormal—and in Chicago—to my late father, who died just weeks after I began college soon after my eighteenth birthday.

When I was a child, like many of my peers, I hated school. Luckily for me, my mother went back to work as a Chicago Public

School teacher when I began kindergarten, and my father took early retirement from the Chicago Police Department to care for me before and after the half-day school program. My father had hated school, too. Moreover, he loved my company and preferred to have me spend my days with him than with my teachers and classmates at St. Benedict Elementary School, and so I rarely went. When the inevitable inquiries came from teachers, the school secretary and, later, the principal, Adalbert Stanislaus Bielski—gruff, loud, and more than a bit intimidating—would scare them off for days or weeks at a time, with my mom none the wiser. I still have the report cards from those days: 14, 27, 45 days and more absent, and I smile when I remember the distinctive education that my dad provided on those days. They were spent decidedly afoot; indeed, I credit my dad with introducing me to the Chicago I grew to adore, as well as to some of the city's most famous ghosts.

One of the places we frequented was Graceland Cemetery, the breathtaking ossuary at Clark Street and Irving Park Road, just up the street from Wrigley Field. When I was eight, my dad taught me to drive there, sitting me up on a phone book in the green Duster so I could see over the wheel. If I did well, he would reward me by taking me to the grave of little Inez Clarke—the enigmatic ghost girl believed to still play among the graves on stormy afternoons—and to view the foreboding statue of *Eternal Silence*—the hooded figure who guards the grave of Chicago magnate, Dexter Graves.

Many days, my dad and I would visit relatives and friends in the old neighborhoods where he'd worked and lived. Stories of the supernatural were always close at hand. Sometimes we'd visit the old Maxwell Street Police Station, from where he'd retired, and the desk sergeant would tell me stories of the screaming they still heard at night from the notorious old basement lockup, where inmates had died by the dozens when the district was one of the bloodiest in the world. Some days we spent time with old buddies in Albany Park, where my dad had attended Transfiguration

Photograph by the author

As a child, one of my favorite sites at Graceland Cemetery was the statue of "Eternal Silence," known as "The Statue of Death."

Photograph courtesy of Eva Cowan

As a girl, I was haunted, figuratively, by the ghost of little Inez Clarke, said to haunt her statue at Graceland Cemetery.

School as a boy and where—one dreadful afternoon at the age of twelve—he had seen what he described as a devil's tail hanging from the bedroom window of the family home.

On a freezing fall morning one year, my dad introduced me to Chicago's most famous phantom, Resurrection Mary. Most researchers, most ghost hunters, most documenters of her life and afterlife have met the elusive Mary in magazine articles, newspaper clippings, or—classically—around a campfire in hushed tones. I met her on a barstool at the tender age of five, drinking a Shirley Temple at Chet's Melody Lounge at 11 A.M. on a Wednesday morning when I was supposed to have been in school. I think this is why, twenty-five years later, I became enchanted by one particular incarnation of our most precious Rez Mary: a twelve-year-old South Side girl named Anna Norkus. Like me, Anna was also a second-generation Eastern European American Chicagoan. Like me, she loved life and music and dancing. And, from a very young age, Anna was (like me) her father's best friend.

The summer before my dad's death, I happened to be home the July afternoon that the phone call came from my Aunt Jessie. Jessie was the longtime girlfriend of my dad's twin brother, Andrew. The two lived alone—well, with a poodle named Dolly—above Jessie's elderly mother at the top of a treacherously steep staircase on Erie Street, near Grand Avenue. This particular afternoon, Andrew had gone across the street to repair a window in one of the apartment buildings they owned on the block. An unfortunate—and frankly unknown—series of events ended in Andrew's three-story fall from the window and the frantic phone call to my dad from Jessie.

My family immediately headed to Northwestern Memorial Hospital where the paramedics had rushed Andrew, but my dad didn't seem to be in much of a hurry. When we asked why he wasn't more upset, Dad said simply, "He's already dead."

In fact, Andrew had actually spoken to my dad on the telephone *after* the accident, claiming that he was fine, swearing like a sailor, and insisting that he didn't need to go to the hospital. Despite his animated response to the fall; however, we did find out—hours later—that Andrew had died in the ambulance on the way to Northwestern. Only my dad—his identical twin—could have known.

Six months later, in early December, my mom and dad were watching television in the living room of the house on Bell Avenue when—from out of nowhere—my dad turned to Mom and said, "My brother's at the door." My mom just looked at him then calmly stated, "Andrew is dead."

My dad didn't respond at first, but crossed his arms and continued watching T.V. A minute later, he said it again, "Lory, I'm telling you, my brother's at the door."

My mom, patient, rose and crossed to the foyer. Opening the front door, she checked the porch and stairs and returned to the couch. "You must be hearing things," she said. "A branch against the glass, the air in the storm windows."

"I'm telling you," he replied, "Andrew is at the door, and he's come for me."

Though the incident passed, a day later my dad took me for a ride on Lake Shore Drive, stopping at Montrose Point, where we used to fish sometimes when I was little. We sat on the rocks that early December afternoon, and the sun was really bright. Just before we got up to leave, he turned to me and said, "I want you to know that I'm going to die. And that it's okay. Don't you worry, Annie."

Now Anne is my given name. Ursula is actually my middle name, but the one that I've used since I was twelve. When I began going by my middle name, my Dad—who had been opposed to such an ethnic name when I was born—was one of the first people to consistently call me "Ursula." He hadn't called me Annie for years, but now here it was again.

I think I called him a fool and told him to stop it. At seventy-two, he was in nearly perfect health and without any reason to suspect the end.

We went home.

The next day, my dad stumbled in the kitchen and fell against one of the tall, old, iron radiators, hurting his ribs. Thinking he had bruised them, he decided to stay in bed for a day or two while he recovered. Two days later, he walked down the stairs to open the door for my mom and collapsed in the front hall. As it turned out, he had broken two ribs, one of which had punctured his lung, causing internal bleeding. Less than a week after the knock on the window, my dad had passed away.

Photograph courtesy of David Cowan

**The Maxwell Street Police Station,
where I heard many of my first ghost stories.**

I.

Negative Space

The skyscraper... has a soul.

—Carl Sandburg
Chicago Poems

C hicago's progressiveness has always been coupled with an awe of the spiritual, likely born of the fact that the city has always been caught between two great natural forces: Lake Michigan to the east and the seemingly endless Midwestern prairie to the west. These awesome presences have certainly inspired Chicagoans to make a mark here, to create a city as natural and as grand as the water and the grass. Chicago architects have been the most influential of the modern age, but their sensible designs have some strange stories to tell. In fact, some of the city's most haunted places are the striking structures concocted by its most controversial designers, from those who built early on, in stone, to the contemporary members of Chicago's most prestigious firms.

In the nineteenth century, when Chicago was burgeoning, no stone was more appealing than our local limestone. Hailing from the region just southwest of the city, Lemont (or Joliet) limestone became one of the most desirable building materials in the nation; its buttery yellow hue and softness of appearance joined with a stability that made the stone irresistible to many builders in Chicago, including architects who designed some of Chicago's most recognizable—and haunted—structures.

On the north side of the city, the Ravenswood Avenue gate of Rosehill Cemetery, designed in limestone by architect W.W. Boyington, is said to be haunted by Boyington's granddaughter, Philomena, who loved to play at the construction site during her short life, cut down by childhood illness. On the south side, the sturdy, limestone Church of St. James-Sag Bridge marks the southernmost point of Chicago's Archer Avenue, one of the most

Photograph courtesy of Angela Larson

**The limestone gate to Rosehill Cemetery
is said to be haunted by the architect's granddaughter.**

haunted roadways in the world... and the burial site of many Irish immigrant workers who, during the mid-nineteenth century, died along the building route of the Illinois and Michigan Canal. Downtown, Holy Name Cathedral, seat of the Catholic Archdiocese of Chicago, is a limestone beauty—marred only by several bullet holes in the cornerstone that remain from the 1926 shooting of North Side Mob leader, Hymie Weiss. Despite repeated efforts of cathedral staff to plug the holes with fresh mortar, the plugs refuse to stick, and mysterious photographs of ghostly orbs at the cornerstone seem to support a paranormal dimension of the site's notoriety.

Doubtless, the most iconic of Chicago's Lemont limestone structures is the Chicago Water Tower, enduring emblem of the city and, indeed, one of the only structures to survive the Great Chicago Fire of 1871. The fire swept Chicago on the night of October 8, hastened by high winds and fueled by kindling from the bone-dry prairie that hadn't seen rain for weeks. More

Photograph courtesy of Michael Spudic

**Limestone giant: Holy Name Cathedral, where bullet holes
still mar the cornerstone from the murder of Hymie Weiss.**

than eighteen thousand buildings were destroyed by the inferno, leveling the city and making way for Chicago's progressive city planners to lay out the 1909 Plan of Chicago: the grid system that made Chicago one of the most sensible cities ever constructed, along with the miles of open public lakefront that made it one of the most beautiful.

And beautiful it is. Today, the Water Tower holds its own along the Magnificent Mile, the glamorous stretch of Michigan Avenue which each year draws millions of shoppers and sightseers from all over the world. In the midst of the glitz, the Tower is a reminder of all that was lost in the fall of 1871… and all that survives. Since the rebuilding of the Near North Side, passersby have frequently glimpsed the apparition of a man hanging in one of the windows of the Chicago Water Tower. Paranormal researchers in Chicago are uncertain about the origin of the apparition, but

Photograph courtesy of David Cowan

**Chicago's Water Tower, one of the only buildings to survive
The Great Fire. The Hancock Building is to the left.**

it's likely that the phenomenon stems from the days after the fire itself, when Chicagoans lived under martial law. In the wake of the fire, looting and further burning became the order of the day, inspiring a curfew and a decree that anyone who did not answer to police should be shot—or hanged—immediately.

Since 1871, historians, journalists, and others invested in Chicago's history have been confounded by the lack of historical documentation before the year of the fire. In fact, almost all of the city's historical records—public and private—were destroyed that October. Some of the first historical records we have are letters written to family and friends in other parts of the country—or overseas—by distraught Chicagoans sending word of survival and death to their loved ones. Though the "official" history of the city denies it, we know from these letters, today nestled safely with the Chicago Historical Society, that many Chicagoans were shot and hanged in accordance with the temporary orders in place immediately after the fire. It seems likely that any ghosts at the event's signature structure must certainly be tied to the chaos of those days, and it may be that the building's handsome limestone itself helps to harbor the memories—or something else.

According to Southwest Side native and paranormal researcher Ed Shanahan, early immigrants without families to care for their remains—including a number of the Irish Illinois and Michigan Canal workers—were cremated rather than buried. Where were the ashes disposed of? The Lemont quarries.

Despite the staying power of Holy Name Cathedral, the gate of Rosehill Cemetery, and the Chicago Water Tower, the city's architectural—and supernatural—renown reaches far beyond these early stone structures.

The Chicago School of architecture was a movement which introduced to architecture steel-frame construction and the use of glass walls. This revolutionary method allowed the creation of much taller—yet more beautiful—buildings. Chicago's Home Insurance Building (1885) was the first to utilize this design, and it wasn't long before Chicago architect Louis Sullivan ran with the concept, realizing the economy of space—and real estate—that the skyscraper would mean. The Chicago School won over many early architects, and Chicago's Loop still shines with their beautiful structures, which remain some of the most inhabitable and defining of the city. The Monadnock, the Marquette, the Board of Trade—these pioneer skyscrapers paved the way for the Amoco Building, the diamond-topped headquarters of Stone Container Building, and of course, the Sears Tower, all key players in Chicago's peerless skyline. But, while at times stunningly beautiful, some of these more modern structures have proved breathtaking indeed... in more sinister ways.

In urban areas around the world, architecture's brilliant progress has been checked by many faults. For every successful design, there are ten that fail—aesthetically, financially, or environmentally. Most troublesome have been the so-called "sick buildings" that have caused everything from nausea and headaches to brain tumors and cancer, due to difficulties with exhaust and ventilation systems, mold growth, and other quirks. In Chicago, one of the most controversial buildings in this birthplace of skyscrapers is believed by Chicago paranormal experts to have a much more malicious quality. Since its completion in 1968, the John Hancock Center has been the site of multiple murders, suicides, and deadly "accidents." Why? Windy City occultists are convinced that it is the very design of the place that causes its residents and workers to often take a turn for the worst.

The John Hancock Center was designed as a trapezoidal structure by its chief architect, Bruce Graham, under the counsel of Fazlur Khan, a structural engineer at the esteemed Chicago

Photograph by the author

Ground-breaking structure… or gateway to another world?
The Hancock Center.

firm of Skidmore, Owings & Merrill. Khan proposed the shape as an economical way to combine larger office spaces on the lower floors with smaller apartment units on the upper levels. It wasn't long before some Chicagoans began to question the "innocent" trapezoidal design as a poor one. Was the building's form, in fact, the shape of things to come?

A little over three years after the Hancock's completion, a twenty-nine-year-old Chicago woman named Lorraine Kowalski fell to her death from her boyfriend's ninetieth-floor Hancock Center apartment. To this day, detectives are dumbfounded by the event; the building's windows are capable of withstanding more than two hundred pounds of pressure per square foot and winds of more than 150 miles per hour, yet Kowalski actually broke through the glass. Four years later, a transmitter technician for a local radio station plunged to his death from the ninety-seventh-floor offices of his television station. Just three months later, a twenty-seven-year old tenant "fell" from his ninety-first-floor apartment while studying for an exam at breakfast. In 1978, a thirty-one-year-old woman shot a man to death in his home on the Hancock's sixty-fifth floor, and in 1998, beloved comedian Chris Farley was found dead in the entrance hall of his sixtieth-floor apartment. Most recently, in March of 2002, a twenty-five-foot aluminum scaffold fell from the building's forty-third floor, crushing three cars, killing three women, and injuring eight others. All of these incidents were called by detectives and journalists "baffling," "inexplicable," and "seemingly unmotivated."

Many years before construction on the Hancock began, the area it would occupy was part of the most luxurious residential district in the city, the Gold Coast. This neighborhood, still known as Streeterville, was already thought to be a cursed tract of land. Cap Streeter was a ragtag former sea captain who made a living ferrying passengers between Chicago and Milwaukee on a beat up old schooner he owned with his wife. After the vessel literally washed up on the Chicago shore during a storm, Cap decided to settle down in the city for good. He staked claim to the very parcel of land on which he had run ashore: prime lakefront property much in demand by Chicago's first families. Cap found the land so lovely that he decided to share the beauty. He set up shop in the old Tremont Hotel, selling tracts of "his" land to willing buyers. Soon a legion of squatters peppered the lakefront, angering Chicago's elite and the city council that served them. When the city repeatedly tried to run off the trespassers, Cap and company responded with shotguns, batons and all manner of homemade weapons.

The battle over "Cap's" land—which he called Streeterville—raged until the man's dying hour... and beyond. On his deathbed, Cap cursed "his" land and swore that no one would ever be happy on it again. Then is the "Curse of Cap Streeter" the source of the Hancock's problem?

Not likely. But it can't help.

In 1930, a baby boy was born in his family's posh home in the 800 block of Chicago's North Michigan Avenue, the same block the Hancock would someday occupy. Musically gifted, Anton Szandor LaVey grew to enjoy a colorful career with many facets, playing in nightclubs and even taming lions for a time. On a spring night in the 1960s, LaVey brought some like-minded friends together, ceremoniously shaved his head, and founded what he called the "Church of Satan," an institution that was part religion, part philosophy, and all based on his own extensive ideas about love, hate, pleasure, and will.

When occultists like LaVey saw the plans for the Hancock revealed, they were devastated. The problem? Not necessarily one for the city itself, but for the residents and workers of the Hancock structure.

LaVey wrote many essays during his time as the satanic church's leader, including fascinating analyses of the problems of modern architecture. LaVey knew—as most occultists do—that the trapezoidal shape holds significant power for arcane forces: traditionally, the shape is believed to serve as a doorway or "portal" for occult—or even diabolical—forces. As a young man,

LaVey was fascinated with the thought of H.P. Lovecraft, whose horror novels often feature characters grappling with the dangers of "strange angles," and it was Lovecraft's work which led LaVey to first pursue his study of modern architecture's sometimes deadly capabilities.

The Hancock Center offers both apartments and offices, and all of the apartments are on the outer edge of the structure, wrapping around the outside as in any other such building. Unfortunately, in the Hancock, every one of these apartments has, due to the trapezoidal structure of the building, an outer wall that is "off-kilter" because it does not rise at 90 degrees. Many—LaVey among them—have believed that these "strange angles" have caused residents of the Hancock to behave in strange and deadly ways, and that the superhuman strength of those who have forced themselves or others through the building's seemingly impenetrable windows were calling on a ready supply of supernatural energy in the Hancock itself: energy coming through the "portal" of its trapezoidal structure.

Students of popular culture will want to note three intriguing legends about the Hancock. First, the structure's legend reportedly inspired Harold Ramis' Hollywood dream of a diabolical building: the centerpiece of his film *Ghostbusters*. Second, the late Heather O'Rourke, myth-shrouded star of the *Poltergeist* films, reportedly took a turn for the worst after a final publicity plug... held in one of the Hancock's studios. Third, a number of controversial or distressed personalities have called the Hancock home, among them, talk show host Jerry Springer, Catholic priest and controversial novelist Andrew Greeley, and—as mentioned—comedian Chris Farley, whose time in the building was riddled with drug and alcohol abuse, the eventual cause of his death.

Bruce Graham was not the first Chicago engineer to see death enter into one of his designs. Generations before, the enduringly popular Frank Lloyd Wright completed Taliesin, his country bungalow home in Spring Green, Wisconsin—a couple of hundred miles northwest of Chicago on the Wisconsin River.

In the summer of 1914, while Wright was away on business in Chicago, Wright's cook sat the family down to lunch, locked all the doors and windows, set fire to the house, and, with a hatchet, murdered six people in the dining room and the screened porch, including Wright's mistress, Mamah Cheney, and her two small children.

Today, Taliesin is a main feature of Spring Green's tourism industry, but the kindly and passionate guides of Wright's masterpiece won't talk about the ghosts that remain after the horrifying events of 1914. Visitors, though, have often smelled the scent of gasoline or smoke in the dining room and sunporch, and occasionally a ghost hunter will illicitly snap a photo which reveals strange patterns of light or misty formations. Children visiting the gorgeous bungalow, too, will sometimes tell of seeing other children in all areas of the house and outside in the garden always described as "wearing funny clothes."

While death has not visited the structures of all of Chicago's great architects, many of these artists have passed over to meet it. An extraordinary gathering of them can be found in Graceland Cemetery, one of the city's loveliest. Here lies William LeBaron Jenney, inventor of the steel skeleton frame and, hence, the first skyscraper. With him, Daniel Burnham, designer of the Columbian Exposition's "White City" and the Plan of Chicago. Louis Sullivan is here, too, his gravestone decorated with lacy metalwork reminiscent of Sullivan's own gorgeous work; nearby rests Richard Nickel, a photographer who was killed while trying to rescue pieces of Sullivan's work during the demolition of the Chicago Stock Exchange building. The list goes on and on to include some of the most prominent contemporary architects: Ludwig Mies van der Rohe, Laszlo Moholy-Nagy, and the Hancock's Fazlur Khan.

While few traditional ghost stories survive at Graceland, Chicago ghost hunters are convinced that something does: this ossuary is one of the most frequented by area investigators. One of their points of pilgrimage is a foreboding monument over the grave of hotel owner Dexter Graves. The bronze statue—named

"Eternal Silence" by Lorado Taft, its sculptor—was long ago nicknamed "The Statue of Death" by Chicagoans. According to legend, a look into the eyes of the hooded shadowy face will reward the viewer with a glimpse of his own demise. Though ghost hunters don't usually come here for a premonition of death, they do take many photos of "Death" because of the orbs and other phenomena that favor the monument, and of the underground tomb of Ludwig Wolff, said to be guarded by Wolff's green-eyed phantom hound.

Feeling depressed by architecture? Don't be. In the South Loop slumbers the striking but peaceful home of the John Glessner family, one of Chicago's most prominent, Victorian-era clans. The house was designed by architect Henry Hobson Richardson, one of the city's most beloved designers, and this would be his final job.

After Richardson's passing, the Glessner family believed—as many still do—that the architect loved this last structure so much that he returned here after death… and remains. From time to time, visitors to Glessner House (now a popular museum in the storied Prairie Avenue District) will encounter a kindly man in its hallways who speaks with great authority and love of the noble home: its careful planning, its architect's struggles to perfect it, its completion at last. When these same visitors comment to the site manager on the friendliness and knowledge of the guide in the hall, the museum staff simply smiles.

II.

The Ghastly Outdoors

You will need to be brave and to go into the woods. It is dark and cold, close and damp... Your feet will bleed. If the dead drink the blood, they will be able to speak to you, but they will not come back with you.

—Veronica Schanoes
How to Bring Someone Back from the Dead

*O*ne of my favorite subjects is the haunted outdoors; that is, haunted roads, forests, bridges, and other spots encountered in the mysterious world outside the safe ones we create for ourselves. Growing up in Chicago, we were drawn to the Forest Preserves that cover surprising acreages of the city. Here, we found escape from the streets to be sure, but more than this, we found a truly magical world where anything could happen... and often did.

The first two Chicago Haunts books explored some of Chicago's most famous outdoor hauntings—Archer Avenue, Robinson Woods, Bachelors Grove—but there are so many more that have been whispered about for generations but have gone undocumented... until now.

On The Road Again: More of Chicago's Paranormal Paths

Around the world for centuries, weary travelers have reached their destinations with tales of haunted roads: white-faced testimonies to encounters with phantom cars and vanishing wayfarers, demonic animals darting across their paths, and spectral trains that cut off their progress, piercing the night with their otherworldly whistles.

Just before Halloween of 2006, the *London Evening Standard* named the ten most haunted roads in Britain. Topping the list was the so-called M6, an ancient highway where Roman soldiers and a ghost truck habitually run drivers off the wayside. In the United States, no road offers up more ghosts per mile than storied Route 66, though cities across the land offer their own contenders.

In New Orleans, the hands-down winner is Canal Street where it meets City Park Avenue, an intersection where no less than thirteen cemeteries join. At one time, the New Basin Canal ran right through this intersection; according to New Orleans history, many of the immigrant canal workers died along the building route and were simply buried where they toppled over from starvation, dehydration, exhaustion, or disease. Today, phantoms are the norm here, from ghost buses and eerie voices to classic apparitions of a woman in white.

It isn't surprising that highways and byways should endure as some of the world's most actively haunted sites, because roads themselves are liminal places. Parapsychologist George Hanson has written extensively about the idea of liminality in the study of paranormal experience. Liminality refers to transitional states, and a number of paranormal researchers have found that liminal places and states foster paranormal experience. Stairs, elevators, even thresholds—these are all places where paranormal events are most often experienced. Liminal places can cause us to feel ungrounded or displaced for a moment or two, perhaps causing us to dispose briefly of our learned sensibilities, perhaps opening our minds for a moment to experiences we normally shut out of our grounded lives.

Roads, then, may fit nicely into this theory. Certainly, traveling ungrounds us and forces us to transition, sometimes for many hours or even days, creating a sort of suspended liminal experience. When the aptly-named "road trip" has the power to change our lives and our relationships, it shouldn't surprise us that such trips often reveal wondrous things, literally along the way.

In Chicago, no road speaks to this idea like Archer Avenue, an old Indian trail which snakes southwest from the city out of the storied Bridgeport neighborhood. The first of the *Chicago Haunts* books keenly explored Archer, a road built over the old trail in the 1830s by Irish immigrants who constructed the Illinois and Michigan Canal, a waterway which burrowed through a major portage to link the Great Lakes and the Mississippi River. The slave-like conditions of their labor, their many deaths from hunger, disease and violence, the cemeteries that sprung up here to take in their bodies, these joined what many feel was—and is—a natural supernaturalism of the road to create one of the most legendary haunted highways in the world, a highway which hosts, among other phenomena, the peerless spirit of Resurrection Mary.

In fact, even psychologists believe that the experience of Mary may be directly related to the road itself. They suggest that it is the hypnotic effect of the darkened road and the repetitive flash of cemetery fences along much of the route that causes travelers to enter into a trancelike state of waking dreaming.

This is, of course, a skeptic's theory.

Believers may wonder, though, if drivers enter into a liminal state along roads like Archer simply because they are unsettling, foreboding, ungrounding. Does this liminal state almost literally pave the way for glimpses of things that are really there, including our elusive Mary?

Chicago Haunts also shared tales of Barrington's infamous Cuba Road, an old highway once used by Prohibition-era gangland travelers between Chicago and Elgin, which speak of phantom cars and houses, mysterious balls of light, the ghosts of lantern-bearing old women, and the eerie mists of fabled White Cemetery. There are a number of other Chicago area roads that give these byways a run for their money.

A Ghosthunter's Stomping Grounds: Shoe Factory Road

This lonely stretch that runs from New Sutton Road east to West Higgins Road in Hoffman Estates is a mystical place with few travelers to attest to its wonders. Those that dare to traverse it tell of phantom children seen running through the adjacent woods, believed to be victims of a long-ago epidemic in the early town of Hoffman. Farther ahead, mysterious lights illuminate the windows of a dilapidated barn of which folklore tells a chilling tale. According to the legend, in the early 1990s, an escaped convict used the barn as a hideout then killed the farm owners when he was discovered... by hanging them one by one in the barn.

Unsettling, yes, but keep driving.

A bit farther on, an abandoned house still stands where, say the locals, a young boy stabbed his parents with an army knife in the late 1960s. According to rumor, you can sometimes see the boy playing with a knife on the house's front steps. Passing by, drivers have reported fresh roses scattered in their paths or the nauseatingly intense smell of them enrobing the car.

It is likely that the stories about the killings at the road's old farmhouse date from 1979 when, on a winter's night in January, a couple and their grown son were slain in their isolated farmhouse on Old Higgins Road, just off Shoe Factory Road southwest of Barrington Road. Earl Teets, a heavy equipment operator and farmer, his wife, Elizabeth, and their son Gary were found shot to death in the house, along with one of their dogs. The foul play by home invaders was discovered by the Teets' second son.

In September of the same year, a barn on the property burned to the ground, but the *Chicago Tribune* chalked this up as one of many such incidents along the "arson-plagued road."

A Bloody Mess in Cherry Valley

Bloods Point Road is the star of a confounding mess of folkore circulated in the desolate Cherry Valley region near Rockford, far northwest of Chicago. Bloods Point Road runs between the Boone County Line on the west and Pearl Street Road on the east. Pearl Street Road, Sweeney Road, Poole Road, Bloods Point Road, Bloods Point Cemetery, Cherry Valley Road, Flora Church Road, and the bridges and rail crossings that dot them: these names all figure in the supernatural world of Bloods Point. It has been suggested that the man-made electromagnetic (EM) fields in this area (i.e. an inordinate number of power lines and electrical towers) may explain the prevalence of paranormal manifestations in the area.

Many have experienced the phenomena associated with this deeply haunted region—like the wandering dead of Bloods Point Cemetery and the hanging girl seen on the bridge at Poole Road, which we'll visit later. But this entire area—especially Bloods Point Road itself—is most paranormally infamous for a phantom car or carriage which runs drivers and pedestrians off the road in the black of night and the light of day. Those brave enough to continue on to where Sweeney Road becomes Poole are then pursued by a ghost *truck* which follows on its heels and then dissipates into a swarm of red lights. Some locals believe that these apparitions have actually caused recent accidents in the area, like the October 2003 deaths of three DeKalb residents.

The victims were traveling north in a Mitsubishi on Cherry Valley Road when an oncoming car attempted to pass a semitrailer truck and a limousine about a quarter mile south of Bloods Point Road. The illegal passing attempt forced the victims' car to veer out of its way, causing it to spin out of control and into the path of the truck. Both the victims' Mitsubishi and the semi burst into flames; everyone in the car was killed, and the suspect's car fled into the night, never to be found.

Almost certainly, it's no phantom that causes accidents like these along dark stretches of road like those in Cherry Valley, but the fact that the connections are mentioned at all suggests a well-defined—and well-founded—fear of vehicle accidents along these roads, a fear given voice by local folklore but also backed-up by ongoing, inexplicable paranormal experiences.

One witness described a recent experience during a night-time excursion to Bloods Point Cemetery with his brother in search of—among other legends—the phantom car or carriage of Bloods Point Road, which is, in fact, most often seen on Pearl Street Road just south of Bloods Point. After their visit, they found themselves traveling on Pearl Street Road toward the railroad crossing. As they passed the tracks, his brother yelled out, claiming to have seen the image of a man standing on the rails. As they slowed the car to turn and look back, a pair of what appeared to be headlights appeared behind them, and the two glimpsed the form of an old-fashioned carriage hurtling towards them, lit not by headlights but lamplights. According to the two witnesses, they were pursued at a breakneck pace back to Bloods Point Road. When they turned west on Bloods Point, the carriage followed, only to disappear into thin air after the car crossed Stone Quarry Road. The witnesses estimated that the carriage had been keeping their pace of about eighty-five mph.

Jack A. Mueller (known as "JAM" on the Haunted Heartland forum he hosts) has encouraged forum members to record such stories and theories of the Bloods Point region. After living in the Bloods Point area for a decade—and hearing about its hauntings from scores of witnesses—Mueller theorizes that "there was a haunting type event that occurred (or is still occurring) somewhere in the area, but that... will most likely remain a mystery to our dying days." Muddling the confusion, he believes, is the fact that

> *...the curious visit the area in expectation of having a paranormal experience. They focus on having such so intensely that ordinary occurrences are interpreted as extraordinary; normal is transformed into paranormal. These personal experiences are also relayed from one person to another. It's the Telephone Game all over again.*

Mueller's own forum has actually gone a long way toward halting this longtime problem. As he himself reasons:

> *Nowadays, in regards to the Bloods Point area, the Internet is very useful in preserving personal experiences as they are being first told to the public. Relaying these in the form of written text instead of word of mouth reduces the potential of distortion(s).*

Still, Mueller admits, we have to rely on ourselves as the best watchdogs; we have to look critically at our experiences with Bloods Point—and all things paranormal—to evaluate them sensibly, regardless of our desire for them to be truly inexplicable:

> *I've debunked my own experiences at the Bloods Point Cemetery involving light anomalies showing up in a series of photographs I took, one of which appeared as a mobile human shape during the daytime. It was actually sunlight traveling down through the trees surrounding the cemetery and striking the shadowed wall of the maintenance shed. There have been many similar reports of 'figures of light' being witnessed roaming about in this cemetery. My best guess is: this is likewise a trick of the moonlight traveling through the trees and striking an object such as a grave marker or patch of mist.*

Still, while Mueller tries to talk some sense into local beliefs about enigmatic Bloods Point, he doesn't have much company. Clearly, the longtime magic of the area—until lately, completely undocumented—casts a spell over most, who return again and again to experience its mysteries, at least in their imaginations. As Mueller so elegantly states, "This area is haunted more so by the living than the dead. And that's what makes Bloods Point so fascinating."

Belief and Ritual: Munger Road

The three-mile highway near St. Charles called Munger Road has been masked in mystery for generations. Munger is the thread that ties together a ghost-infested region that, today, is one of the most suburban you'll find. But decidedly un-suburban residents populate this road, including a red-eyed wolf and a red phantom Oldsmobile, just two of the many ghosts that have been reported on this byway, rumored to run through "devil-worshipper country," where children are routinely sacrificed in an abandoned silo nearby.

Don't believe it?

You may want to reconsider. Phantom cars and dogs are often glimpsed at sites that have become locations of ritual activity. Places often become sites of ritual activity because of stories of hauntings, and Munger Road and its environs own several classic hauntings that have long endured. According to very old legends still claimed today, the railroad tracks on Munger replay a devastating event from a century ago.

As it is told, three children who lived in a farmhouse up the road were playing along the rails with their baby sister resting in a carriage nearby. When it was time to go home to supper, the children headed for their house across the tracks, wheeling the carriage over them. When one of the carriage wheels became stuck in a twisted piece of rail, the children panicked; a train was fast approaching. Desperately, the children pushed the carriage from behind, heaving against the canvas-covered frame. In the nick of time, the wheel came free, and the carriage slipped ahead. Tragically, in their effort, the children lost their balance and went sprawling across the tracks, where they were killed by the oncoming train. When the parents of the children arrived at the scene, they found the engineer's story backed up by the dirty handprints of the children on the back of the baby's carriage. Tales are still told that if you drive onto these tracks today, the car will stall. Though you will not be able to start it again, an unknown force will gently scoot the car over the rails, and the imprint of tiny hands will be found on the car's dusty trunk. Travelers along Munger have also reported seeing a little boy running along the side of the road, but when they turned around to see if the boy needed help, they found he had vanished.

In some versions of this legend, the accident at the tracks occurred in the mid-twentieth century, when a school bus full of children stalled on the Munger Road tracks, leading to the death of the children and the derailing of the train—which plowed right through several adjacent houses, killing a number of residents at home. Though the details are different, the handprints remain as the central part of the story. Even today, with the tracks no longer in operation, witnesses claim that cars stopped on the tracks will be gently pushed over by the invisible little hands of the vanquished passengers of that ill-fated bus ride.

Similar stories are told around the world, usually at train tracks where school bus accidents have occurred. Often, these sites share tales of cars that stall on the tracks, only to be helped across by tiny hands that leave their telltale prints behind. The most famous version—and some say the inspiration for the others—hails from San Antonio, Texas, and has been excellently investigated by renowned paranormal researcher Bill Knell. Historically, in 1949 a school bus filled with children found its engine stalling as it tried to climb a small grade just past the tracks of a rail crossing at the Shane and Villamain Roads, just off of San Antonio's Southeast Loop 410. Though the bus was able to get its front wheels over the rails, the back wheels became lodged in the rails and, because of the steep grade on the other side, the wheels could not be worked free, and the engine continued to stall. When an approaching train appeared, several of the children were able to escape through the windows, but the driver of the bus and most of the children on board perished.

Not longer after the accident (which led to nationwide changes in railroad and school bus safety policies), the ghosts of some of the children began to be seen by those living near the tracks, and, as the years passed, it became known that a car stalled on the dangerous tracks would be pushed over and up the grade on the other side—by invisible hands that would leave their little prints in the dusty trunks or bumpers.

I learned about the secrets of Munger Road from Chris Gaulding, who I found through Jamie Clemons, host of the well-known and wonderful Jamie's Chicago Gangsterland Ghost Pages. Gaulding, who grew up in the Chicago area and now lives in Houston, spent a number of years working for the Forest Preserve

District of DuPage County. As Munger Road runs through Pratt's Wayne Woods, part of the FPD property, he spent much time on Munger and learned many of the truths behind the old legends:

> *I love the legend of Munger Road, partly because of how I discovered it and the time of my life when it all happened. I worked with the Forest Preserve District, as a Park Ranger. I had access to all properties at all times. I spent many a day patrolling Munger Road, which goes through the middle of Pratt's Wayne Woods. I found out from one of the seasonal workers, a college freshman, that this road was legendary in Chicago, and (that) it was haunted. I laughed. She told me the all the stories... The bus story never happened. I can confirm that with several individuals, old timers who worked in the area for the last twenty-five years. However, the train derailing and smashing all the houses can be confirmed. The two legends I have heard go like this:*

> *1) There was an old man who lived on Munger Road. He was a mean and heartless old fart, and he spooked people out in general. The story is that a train derailed and smashed his house, killing his family. This made him bitter and he would attack and kill you if you went down his road.*

> *2) The train derailed and smashed a number of houses. The truth? There was an old man who lived in a small house on Munger Road. It was situated about fifteen feet from the tracks. He was not mean or heart-less, he was just old and lonely, and these stupid kids kept driving down the street and egging his house and prying around his yard on a nightly basis. The Rangers in the area befriended him and helped him out. His kids had moved away, and he was alone. Many years ago, a train derailed. It slid many yards and came to rest against his*

house, almost pushing the house off its blocks. A catastrophe narrowly escaped: no one was hurt. He died in 1999, and his property (a small yard and house) was left to the Forest Preserve District. Before it was demolished in the spring of 2000, I went into the house and looked around. It was a two room shack, cluttered; the only thing of interest was a card hanging on the refrigerator, probably from a grandchild, a sweet homemade card urging him to get well soon. Kind of heartbreaking when you think about all the stuff that guy went through, but someone still loved him. Now there is the subject of the farmhouse up the road to the north of the tracks. There is not much history in this one. It was an old farm house, (belonging to) the people who owned a lot of the property immediately around it. It was abandoned for several years before I got there. But I think the moment someone moves out of a house like that, it becomes haunted. This one, I can't blame anyone for being creeped out about. You remember The Blair Witch Project? *That house and this one were identical. It stood about fifty to one hundred yards north of the tracks, a two-story white house surrounded by huge oaks. But the truth of the mater is: It was a creepy old house where a fire had occurred. There was a hole in the floor where a fire had ruined the house for its inhabitants, the explanation for the abandonment. There were numerous signs of vandalism and the discarded packages of masks and things which someone had used in a lame attempt to scare someone else. There was nothing haunted about that place. It was also demolished in the spring of 2000. I watched the grounds crew tack it down; it took about four hours with a bulldozer. They left nothing. Maybe next time you go out there you will find the foundation and a tree growing up in the middle of it.*

Munger Road was a creepy place. The old houses in the middle of our modern suburbs lent a real eerie twist to this deserted area. But that is the beauty of the Forest Preserve District. There are a ton of places like that. Go to that area some cool sunny afternoon. Park on the side of the road. Walk up the hill and out into the prairie grass until you can't see the road anymore. From here you should be able to look west and out over the whole preserve. There is where the real supernatural experience will happen to you. God is out there, just enjoying the view. Sit and talk a while.

Stone-cold Haunted: The Ghosts of Gifford Road

Gifford Road lurks in the vicinity of Munger and runs through gravel pits and past a stone quarry. Gifford, a dark road with a storied past, has long been a favorite place for racing at night, and a place where midnight races sometimes go wrong. Longtime locals tell of drag racing on Gifford in the '50s and '60s, when drag racers killed on the road were said to haunt the Bluff City Cemetery. According to local reports—which could not be documented—racers would occasionally veer off the road above the quarry, plunging into the gaping void below.

I visited Gifford Road and the two cemeteries off Bluff City Road in the fall of 2006 and found that, even today, the area is an eerie one. Traveling along the road near sunset, I could almost picture the drag racers I'd heard about making their final runs along the gravel pits and meeting their fates on this all but abandoned stretch. Later, walking in near-darkness among the markers at Bluff City Cemetery, I actually found one section of the burial ground where my thermometer registered drops of more than sixty degrees for several seconds, though I felt no change myself. At home the next week, after developing the film I'd used there, I was delighted to find I'd captured some great shots of Gifford Road, though every shot of Bluff City Cemetery had turned out blank.

"They were both just gone": The Ghosts of Monee Road

Monee Road and intersecting Sangamon Street run carefully through the village of Crete, a place with more than its share of hauntings, some of them right along the way. On Monee Road, a drive over the railroad tracks has brought on for some witnesses the phantom scream of a young girl, often accompanied by her white-robed apparition on the tracks. On Sangamon Street, stormy nights may usher in a similar experience, the vision of a haggard woman and a young boy who appear in the headlights of the car.

One Indiana woman shared with me a particularly unsettling encounter which took place on a hail-battered night in the spring of 2006:

I think it was in April, and I had never been in the area before. I had been golfing with some friends from work and we were about halfway through—at around dinnertime—when this crazy sort of storm broke out and it started to rain. I had left, though my friends had urged me to stay and eat with them, and I was trying to get to the Bishop Ford Freeway. They had sent me east on Old Monee Road with directions on where to turn, but of course I screwed them up. It was a really desolate road where I ended up and almost immediately felt I had made a wrong turn, but even before I reached the next road to look for a sign, a wild-looking woman appeared from what seemed out of nowhere right in the middle of the road, sort of almost dragging a young boy behind her—about seven or eight years old (my son was seven at the time and he looked like he could have been in my son's grade)—and he looked either half-asleep or like he'd been walking for hours and was about to fall down from exhaustion. Well, as you can imagine, I slammed on the brakes, which was not a good thing in the weather, and my car skidded so that it turned almost halfway around. And honestly, by the time I caught my breath—just a few seconds later—they were both just gone. I can tell you this was so shocking—I pulled my car over to the side of the road and rolled down the window but couldn't see anyone around and then actually got out of the car because I was sure I must have hit them both, but there was just no one anywhere. I called 911 on my cell which is how I found out I'd been on the wrong road—they (the police) were driving all over Dixie Highway trying to find my car—and when they found me and I told them what had happened, they didn't seem too concerned and didn't spend much time looking for the people I'd seen.

Night Riders

Along storied Kean Avenue southwest of the city one may still find the odd horse stable, artifacts of the days when the area was peppered with equestrians enjoying the seemingly endless acres of riding paths in this heavily forested realm. Today, most of the old crossings across the now-paved roads are too dangerous for modern riders; indeed, numerous accidents in years gone by continue to keep horse-lovers from these crossings. Victims of one such accident are still said to traverse the crossing which claimed their lives.

On August 3, 1975, a Palos Hills girl was crossing the old equestrian path across Ninety-fifth Street near Kean Avenue when she and her horse were struck by a car driven by a man from nearby Bridgeview. Both the girl and the animal were killed when the horse was thrown twenty-five feet and the girl thirty-five feet.

In recent years, drivers through this old crossing have reported seeing the images of horses and their riders making their way over the modern road, without a sound, and disappearing without a trace. Some link these phantoms to the tragedy of 1975, while others have unearthed another possibility. Chicago-area ghost hunter Richard Crowe (who lives in the area) found that some time ago a nearby stable had been closed down due to the owner's neglect. As a result, many of the stable's horses were put down. The stable was located a mere block from the crossing.

◆

Less than a mile from the ghostly horse crossing at Ninety-fifth Street is another infamous accident sight, this one of legend. The tragedy is said to have occurred near Sacred Heart Cemetery, at 101st Street, in the 1950s when a young couple perished in a crash during an afternoon drive through the Palos preserves. Their baby, unrestrained according to the practices of the time, was thrown from the car into the adjoining woods. Though the families of the couple frantically alerted police about the missing child, an extensive search turned up no trace of the baby.

Years later, reports began to circulate of a strange creature glimpsed by motorists along Kean Avenue—a childlike figure, human in every way except one: a sheen of gray hair covered its entire body. As the years went on, reports of the so-called "Gray Baby" turned to those of the "Kean Avenue Werewolf," presumably after the long-lost child had grown to manhood in the dense preserves of Southwest Chicago. Tales of a hairy man-beast dashing through car headlights joined equestrian accounts of horses spooked by unseen figures on the horse paths.

Some local residents don't believe their local werewolf is the grown up Gray Baby at all but an actual local victim of lacan-thropy (the psychological "werewolf disease") who retreated to the woods years ago to escape the pain of living in normal society. Theorists suggest that, like Gray Baby, years of living unsheltered through the harsh Chicago winters has resulted in the unfortunate lycanthropist's growth of thick body hair—and a physical appear-ance quite suited to his psychological self-perception.

Photograph courtesy of Michael Spudic

**Chicago's laborers, as sculpted on one of the
Michigan Avenue Bridge towers.**

Spanning Realities: Chicago's Haunted Bridges

Around the world, bridges host some of the most amazing paranormal phenomena. Not surprising. Returning to the idea of liminality, what could be more transitional—more liminal—than the crossing of a bridge? Add to this the tendency of the distressed to take their lives at these same sites and you've got a spot that's primed for the preternatural.

One of the nation's most fascinating haunted bridges is the Rio Grande Gorge Bridge near Taos, New Mexico, which spans a twelve-hundred-foot width and a six-hundred-foot depth. The Southwest Ghost Hunters Association (SGHA) investigated the bridge in 2005, lured by repeated reports of apparitional sightings on the west side of the bridge. The apparition—which is most often seen by state troopers—is that of a young Hispanic woman clad in blue jeans and a plain white t-shirt who walks east along the south rail of the bridge, disappearing somewhere near the center. During their investigation, it was along this stretch that SGHA obtained their only significant fluctuations in the electromagnetic (EM) fields, a possible sign that paranormal activity is at work. When the SGHA turned to the local newspaper archives, they found that between September 1990 and June 2003 no less than fifteen documented suicides occurred from the bridge, along with at least one murder, when a driver was thrown from the bridge into the Rio Grande Gorge by carjackers. Among these, not one could be tied to the description of the bridge's apparition, though there may well be an earlier documented—or recent undocumented—suicide that may someday be discovered to back up the paranormal reports.

In Chicago, our most famously haunted bridge is actually two bridges: the Clark Street Bridge and the LaSalle Street Bridge that span the Chicago River. Standing on either of these bridges, countless witnesses have experienced the paranormal residue of the horrific *Eastland* Disaster, the city's deadliest tragedy. When, in July 1915, the *Eastland* steamer overturned on the river between these two bridges, the result was the deaths of more than

Photograph courtesy of Michael Spudic

The Michigan Avenue Bridge, where ghostly soldiers still march.

830 passengers—and a century of paranormal phenomena. Walkers across these structures have made many claims: hearing the sound of splashing in the water, hearing cries for help, sometimes even by name, and of feeling either panicked or strangely drawn to the water.

Just a few minutes' walk east will find strollers at the Michigan Avenue Bridge, site of Chicago's earliest Anglo settlements and of the first Fort Dearborn, which was set on fire by Native American British sympathizers during the War of 1812, taking the lives of a number of American soldiers. This bridge is a place where sightseers will sometimes report apparitions of the defeated troops of Fort Dearborn, marching in formation across the bridge (which, fascinatingly, was not even built at the time of the war).

◆

Axeman's Bridge in Crete is the site of one of the most widely-circulated—and under-documented—urban legends in the Southeastern Chicago area. According to the tale, sometime in the 1970s a local resident took the lives of his wife and children, axing them to death. After the children failed to show up at school for several days in a row, police were dispatched to the house to discover their whereabouts. Upon entering the house, the officers found it empty, with signs of a swift abandonment. Flies fed on plates of food on the kitchen table, the television wailed in the background, and the back door of the house stood open. Following through the door and into the yard, the officers made their way to a shed where, inside, they found the decaying bodies of the family strung up on meat hooks—and the axe-wielding man of the house, who promptly offed the two policemen.

When the officers failed to return to headquarters—or radio a response to repeated calls—a fleet of police was sent to investigate. Upon arrival, officers found the killer preparing to similarly string up his most recent victims. Bolting from the shed through a side door, he fled the scene, pursued through the woods by a dozen officers, one of whom shot and killed the murderer near the bridge which today bears his name.

For years, the house of the Axeman—now demolished—was the site of many pilgrimages. Ghosthunters from Illinois and Indiana traveled to the house to see for themselves the blood-stained shed, the dishes still on the kitchen table, and the path down which the Axeman had fled. Some visitors claimed to have seen the apparition of a woman hanging from a rope in a tree outside the bedroom windows. But the point of most of these travels was to participate in a famous ritual on Axeman's Bridge. Can you guess?

According to the legend, any car that tries to cross the bridge will find its engine sputtering and dying. The cause? Reportedly, the enraged energy of the Axeman, trapped forever at the moment of death, zaps the engines every time. Nothing but a manual push can get you on your way again... or so they say.

◆

The bridge on Bloods Point Road is part of the very haunt-ed—but sketchy—history of the Bloods Point region already discussed. According to legend, part of the haunted past of this desolate Cherry Valley road concerns a school bus which once jumped the bridge rail, leading to the death of every child on board. Many have tested the folktale which claims that a car placed in neutral on the bridge will be pushed to the other side by invisible little hands, similar to the earlier stories told of the Munger Road crossing and the original events which continue in San Antonio, Texas. Though no historical records have been found to support the events at Bloods Point Road, many witnesses claim to have tested the legend, parking on the bridge in neutral, only to have their cars pushed over.

Many have also claimed to have seen apparitions of two men hanging from this bridge, grim reminders of a treacherous event alleged to have happened in the early-twentieth century on the farm that abuts the bridge. According to the story, two farmhands were discovered in the act of raping the farmer's daughter. Enraged but collected, the girls' father fashioned twin nooses for the men and, at gunpoint, forced them to hang themselves from Bloods Point Bridge.

Bloods Point Bridge is not the only haunted bridge of the Bloods Point Region. According to the legend of Ox's Bridge (also known as the Bridge on Poole Road), two separate events are responsible for the preternatural experiences reported here. The first event occurred on a spring evening long ago, when a young farm girl, thwarted on her prom night, made her way to the bridge and hanged herself from it, dressed to the nines. The second event concerns a train that once traveled over the bridge, until it derailed, killing the conductor. According to stories told today, Ox Bridge hosts frequent sightings of a woman hanging from the bridge and of the long-dead conductor, said to be looking for his lost train. Sometimes, the apparition of the conductor is accompanied by the sound of an approaching train, though none is visible.

Of course, residents of the surrounding areas make frequent trips to Ox Bridge in the hopes of an experience of their own. Most of the time, they are disappointed. Occasionally, however, something happens that makes all the midnight trips worthwhile, sometimes sighting a young woman wandering along the road or standing on the bridge in the wee hours. Some researchers in the area believe that a nearby quarry may be partly responsible for these hauntings since certain types of stone seem to have the ability to "harness" energy and hold onto it for years. This has been a common theory in the Chicago area for many years as the limestone mined from many Chicago-area quarries is known as such a material. In fact, many Chicago-area limestone buildings have famous ghost stories associated with them, like the Water Tower, many of the city's old cemetery gates, and Holy Name Cathedral.

♦

On November 16, 2004, a young woman named Nicole Carter was driving to her evening class at Moraine Valley Community College in the Palos region southwest of Chicago. As she traveled along Eighty-seventh Street approaching Roberts Road, Nicole passed over the Eighty-seventh Street Bridge, spanning a line of railroad tracks below. There on the bridge, she saw something that she believes will always haunt her.

"It was a person," Nicole remembers, "wearing a long-sleeved white sweater... like a hoodie." Though Nicole couldn't distinguish the sex of the person, a couple in the car in front of hers did. Later, Nicole would learn that the couple were convinced it had been a woman and had seen "red pants and hair." As Nicole's car—and her future co-witnesses in the car ahead—casually passed, the woman on the bridge did something astounding. She leaned forward, put her arms out to her sides, and—"like purposely falling... like bungee jumping"—plunged elegantly over the side.

Horrified, the two witnessing cars pulled over. Nicole was first to the bridge rail. She recalls, "I knew I would find someone dead." Yet, when she peered over to the tracks below, there was no one there.

The Bridgeview police were called. Nicole recalls that when they arrived, they seemed "not overly excited" about the incident. Later she would learn that this reaction was one that had come from years of investigating the same panicked calls—with the same empty results.

At school that night, Nicole told her best friend what she had seen—what had made her late for class. When her friend told her own mom about the incident, her mom remembered an incident that had occurred not long after the bridge was completed—an incident, yes, of suicide.

Into The Woods

Chicago Haunts readers and Chicago-area ghost hunters are well acquainted with the Native American spirits of Robinson Woods, the enigmatic phenomena of Bachelor's Grove, and the Boy Scout tales of Camp Fort Dearborn, but sites like these are as seemingly endless as the stories that surround them.

In September 1967, a fourteen-year-old Mather High School student accepted a stranger's ride from school to her Northwest Side Chicago home. Several days later, her body was found in a pool of shallow water in the Chicago River running through LaBagh Woods, near Foster and Pulaski. Not long after, walkers through those woods began reporting the sound of singing and the feeling of being watched or followed by unseen eyes. A few witnesses claimed to have seen the young girl standing in the water where her body was found. As the years passed, the preserve became rumored as a center of Northwest-Side cult activity, and soon the earlier phenomena were joined by the apparitions of cloaked figures, choruses of whispers that would follow close behind, and reports of hikers being "chased" by someone they couldn't actually see.

One man, now in his forties, describes his own experience at LaBagh Woods in the summer of 1986:

> *We had gone into the woods around eleven at night—we walked from my friend John's house who lived over by the expressway. We had nothing else to do those days, you know, in high school, all the kids would just hang out at each others' houses and walk around, but we'd always end up in the woods 'cause we could drink there. We used to go down by the river until around two in the morning, and sometimes there would be cops from the Forest Preserve (District). But back then, almost never. This one night, right after we started school in the fall, we had gone in the woods on Friday night and down by the river like we always did, and we had, I don't know, like*

a bag of beers, but we only drank not even one each and then saw this girl in the river. I don't mean like swimming or drowning or anything—just sort of standing in the water, it was only about up to her ankles, which seemed weird because it seemed deeper at the time, and she was wearing kind of a short skirt dress that almost looked like a long shirt. She had this straight dark hair that almost looked liked the Ring *girl, you know, in the movie. It was weird that she was there, especially standing in the water, 'cause it wasn't really warm anymore—we were wearing jackets, I know—but it was really spooky after a minute because she just stood there, not doing anything, and then walked over toward the bank to get out, and we wondered is she gonna come over by us? And of course, guys, we thought, Woo Hoo! But she was gone after that. She went behind some trees and didn't come out the other side, and we thought, what happened? We thought about seeing if she maybe slipped and fell in the water or something, but of course we just left. I think we even left the beer there. Later on, when I was working years later, a cop I knew told me about the girl who had been killed and found there, and it was right where we used to drink. We went back a lot of times before that to hang out, but we never saw her again. Some other kids saw her over the years but didn't know about the killing either.*

♦

Red Gate Woods have long been known as haunted, running as they do along notorious Archer Avenue. It is these woods that shiver with the chanting of an invisible chorus, and these woods that host apparitions of monks seen both here and at the adjacent churchyard of St. James-Sag. It has been ventured that the haunting of Red Gate Woods may be connected to gangland days when neighboring homes and business were joined by long, underground tunnels for use during the Prohibition era. According to some tales, a number of such tunnels ran to still-remote areas like Red Gate Woods from roadhouses as much as a mile away, making it simple work to do away with a rival in the basement and cart off the body for burial in the surrounding as-yet-uncharted woodland.

History may never verify these events, but one other, much stranger reality cannot be denied.

As a child growing up in the deeply forested Palos area southwest of Chicago, acclaimed advocacy writer and environmentalist John James Bell remembers that aimless hikes in the area's seemingly endless preserves were what little boys were made of. But, as Bell recalls in his essay "The Many Faces of Apocalypse," fossils and turtles were not the normal loot such treks revealed, especially one surreal afternoon:

> *As kids, my friends and I stumbled across the old piece of plywood while hiking. Such large junk was a familiar site—these woods on Chicago's South Side near Palos Forest Preserve were really not woods at all but overgrown underbrush along the industrial Illinois and Michigan Canal Corridor. The piece of plywood was almost overlooked, but I noticed that if you jumped on it there was a bit of a bounce. We cleared off the dirt and grass. There were hinges; it was a makeshift door. With some effort we opened it and within seconds we pledged to keep our discovery secret. After all, it's not every day that you find buried in the woods a nuclear fallout shelter...*

This was Red Gate Woods. Before speaking with Bell, I had heard about the woods from Ed Shanahan, an expert on Southwest Side paranormal phenomena, who had informed me, after a lifetime of my unknowing, that the nation's first nuclear reactor was established here in 1943. To this day the reactor reposes under the forested landscape along Archer Avenue. In fact, nuclear engineers from the nearby Argonne National Laboratory are in charge of environmental monitoring of the woods for the U.S. Department of Energy.

Argonne, which sprawls over more than 1500 acres in DuPage County, was the nation's first national laboratory, having been chartered in 1946. Argonne's mission began with the Manhattan Project, the monumental World War II venture which saw its success at the University of Chicago when Enrico Fermi and more than four dozen colleagues accomplished the world's first controlled nuclear chain reaction. When the war ended, Argonne was founded to develop nuclear reactor sites for peaceful use. Red Gate Woods had already been established at the time of Argonne's founding, and the new laboratory was naturally put in charge of it at once. The University of Chicago reactor, known as Chicago Pile-1, was moved after the war to Red Gate Woods to be buried next to Chicago Pile-2, which was developed at Red Gate itself. While the area is consistently declared safe, as Shanahan asserts, there may be "a very good reason why paranormal tools may go a bit out of whack when taken there." As, indeed, they do. In fact, the presence of the reactors may even explain some of the paranormal phenomena experienced here, including apparitional sights and sounds, perhaps given life by the long-buried energy on site.

III.

Staying Awhile

I'm not afraid of werewolves or vampires or haunted hotels. I'm afraid of what real human beings to do other real human beings.

—Walter Jon Williams

*S*o much is experienced by travelers. Open to new experiences and cut free for a day, a week, a month from routine, those away from home seem somehow open to truly alternate realties, especially at the site where they lay down to sleep.

The Sheraton Gateway Suites Hotel in Rosemont is an eleven-story atrium hotel near O'Hare Airport. Like many such buildings, a number of past guests have reportedly committed suicide by throwing themselves over the atrium railings. Since one such incident in the fall of 2001, the victim has been seen—in suit and tie—gazing over the east side of the atrium rail. A number of drug overdose deaths have also occurred here, and in such rooms guests have reported dark figures, disembodied voices, and the dishevelment of their clothes and belongings, often while they are in the bathroom.

The nearby O'Hare Hilton, directly across from the airport entrance, was long rumored to have an "uninhabitable" room—one that just made guests so inexplicably uncomfortable that they literally couldn't sleep.

There's the Baymont Inn and Suites in Aurora, where employees have witnessed balls of white light in the lobby area and where guests are repeatedly driven from room 208 by a spirit who seeks to strangle them in their sleep.

There is the old Leland Park, also in Aurora, haunted by a number of guests who have reportedly checked in, not to stay the night but to throw themselves into the Fox River from this, one of the tallest buildings in the city. Noxious odors and disembodied voices are reportedly rife in the building, now an apartment development.

Photograph courtesy of Angela Larson

The Hotel Florence, grand lady of the Pullman community.

The Hotel Florence, in Chicago's historic Pullman district, is rumored to be haunted by a woman who lived in the hotel at one time, and the hip House of Blues Hotel is home to a number of phantoms, including that of a young girl believed to have died in the building when it was an office complex.

Cubs Fever

Two very different North Side hotels share an unsavory honor, for both hotels witnessed—believe it or not—shootings of Chicago Cubs players. Both are also believed to be haunted though, interestingly, both victims survived.

The erstwhile Edgewater Beach, known fondly to Chicagoans as "The Pink Hotel" was in its heyday one of Chicago's most glamorous destinations. Pretty as a candy box, the rosy beauty sparkled on the very shore of Lake Michigan (its twin, the Edgewater Apartments, still stands today).

The Edgewater Beach was the stage for one of baseball's most bizarre incidents. On May 10, 1949, Ruth Ann Steinhagen attempted to kill the man she had long loved from afar, former

Photograph courtesy of Angela Larson

**The Edgewater Apartments,
twin of the now-demolished Edgewater Beach Hotel.**

Cubs infielder Eddie Waitkus. In the 1980s, the Secret Service dubbed Steinhagen "The Original Stalker," distinguishing her as the model for a very modern new breed, the seemingly normal individual who for some unknown reason becomes violently obsessed with another person. The story of Ruth and Eddie inspired Bernard Malamud to pen his popular novel, *The Natural*, the basis for the much-beloved movie of the same name. Before its demolition, the Edgewater Beach was believed to bear at least a trace of the confrontation between Waitkus and Steinhagen.

It happened in room 1297.

The afternoon of the shooting, Ruth had gone to see the newly-traded Waitkus play for Philadelphia against the Cubs. After the game she made her way to the Edgewater Beach, where she had booked a room knowing that was where Waitkus would be staying. She ordered several drinks from room service and then gave the following note to a bellhop, asking him to deliver it to Waitkus' room:

> *It is extremely important that I see you as soon as possible. We are not acquainted, but I have something of*

importance to speak to you about. I think it would be to your advantage to let me explain this to you as I am leaving the hotel the day after tomorrow. I realize this is out of the ordinary, but as I say, it is extremely important.

Coincidentally, Waitkus had been seeing a young woman by the name of Ruth Martin, and it was not unusual for the two to rendezvous while Watikus was away from home, so he headed up to 1297 to see his girl. When he arrived, Steinhagen was the only one there. When Waitkus asked where Ruth was, she told him she would be back in a moment. As he made his way into the room to sit down, Steinhagen took a .22 caliber rifle from the closet and swiftly shot Waitkus in the stomach saying, "If I can't have you nobody can."

Incredibly, Eddie survived, though the bullet went in under his heart and caused one of his lungs to collapse.

In the first years after the crime, some tenants of Steinhagen's room had reported seeing a tall, attractive brunette sitting on the bed when first entering. Those entering would excuse themselves, thinking they had been given the wrong room number, only to have the young woman respond, "I'm just waiting for someone. I'll be gone soon," as she always was when the intruders returned with the desk clerk. This is an illustrative example of a haunting that stems from a traumatic event but not a deadly one. Though Steinhagen had intended to shoot herself after the killing, she did not. She called the front desk and told the clerk she'd shot a man. Nonetheless, room 1297 seemed to have harbored a definite haunting, an imprint of that shocking night long ago.

♦

On July 6, 1932, the Hotel Carlos, now Sheffield House Hotel, 3834 North Sheffield Avenue, had been the scene of a similar clash between Cubs shortstop Billy Jurges and Violet Valli, a local cabaret singer who had crossed the line from admiring to obsessed. Valli had written a note to her brother, claiming that

Photograph by the author

The Sheffield House today.
Notice the "Go Cubs Go!!" painted on the ground-floor window.

Photograph by the author

The entrance to the Sheffield House Hotel,
where the old Hotel Carlos sign remains.

life wasn't worth living if she couldn't be with her love and that she was going to "leave this earth" and "take Billy with me." Valli never mailed the letter. She drank a good amount of gin, left the letter on her desk, and went to room 509, Jurges' room, where she shot him in the hand and the buttocks.

In March 2008, *Chicago Sun-Times* columnist Dave Hoekstra conducted a séance in room 509, under the mediumship of Rik Kristinant, attempting to contact Jurges about the upcoming Cubs season, the one-hundredth anniversary since the team's last World Series win. Without prior knowledge of the location or the event, Kristinant offered that there had been a shooting in the hand and that the room smelled of lilies of the valley, a psychic indication that a woman had been involved, with a name like Rose or something similar. He also claimed to hear a voice reminiscent of the Bronx, where Jurges was born. The Sheffield House still operates, nearly in the shadow of Wrigley Field.

Death at the Drake

Drivers in Chicago traveling southbound on Lake Shore Drive from the North Side always know when the Magnificent Mile is near. The Drake Hotel's pink neon moniker has lit up the top of Michigan Avenue since the Jazz Age, and its halls have, in fact, been haunted since the first guests arrived.

On its opening night, New Year's Eve 1920, the Drake Hotel hosted an unforgettable gala in the lavish Gold Coast Room, a sumptuous ballroom overlooking the sands of the city's posh Oak Street Beach. All of Chicago was agog over the opulent event, but of the hundreds of well-heeled revelers present, only one is still talked about today: the beguiling but blighted Woman in Red. Don't confuse her with Anna Sage—the *Lady* in Red who ratted out chum John Dillinger in 1939. The Drake's red-garbed woman was the decided victim in her own sorry yarn.

According to legend, the still-anonymous woman—dressed in a red silk ball gown and escorted by her fiancé—had enjoyed that long-ago evening's merry offerings, giddy with delight over her boyfriend's proposal just a week earlier on Christmas Eve. Though the couple shared many dances that evening and tipped numerous cocktails with friends and each other, the woman at some point struck up a conversation with an old friend, and her man excused himself to smoke a cigar in the lobby.

A few minutes later, the orchestra struck the first notes of the couple's favorite song, and the woman quickly left her friend to find her fiancé, hoping to mark the start of their wedding year with a twirl to their beloved tune. Though much time had passed since his departure, a scan through the room revealed no trace of her love. Guessing that he must have met a colleague in the lobby and lingered, she began her way there, preparing to drag him out of the smoke-filled gathering of men and back to the party with her.

Passing the door of the Palm Court tea parlor across the hall, however, she heard the low but unmistakable sound of her lover's voice, and she entered the room to find him. As she wound a path through the elegant tables, she suddenly stopped. A second voice had joined that of her fiancé, a breathy, feminine whisper, punctuated with the tinkle of sly laughter. Continuing through the maze of chairs and potted palms, she finally spotted them in the farthest corner of the room cloaked in shadows and engaged in a kiss.

Without a word, the woman turned from the demoralizing scene. Gathering up the skirts of her scarlet gown, she rushed through the parlor and into the hall, the strains of the orchestra drowning her frenetic sobs. Entering the elevator at the end of the hall, she rode, alone, to the top floor of guest rooms, tearing down the length of them to find the stairs to the roof. A burst of tearful power brought her at last to the top, the freezing air of the year's final night like a slap against her burning cheeks.

There, at the summit of the Drake, she scanned the beauty of the Chicago evening with Lake Michigan to the north and east stretching, it seemed, to the ends of the earth. The natural vista seemed to calm her for a moment until she turned to look southwest. For out there, beyond the twinkling lights of the Loop skyscrapers, lay the home her lover had found for them, the home which was to be theirs and their children's, the home, now, of nothing but nightmares.

Newly stricken, the woman walked calmly to the edge of the roof and, with a final breath, gathered her crimson skirts about her one last time, and stepped off.

Ever since, guests and staff have told many tales of the pitiable Woman in Red. Since her suicide that long-ago night, she has been spotted at each scene of her drama: in the Gold Coast Room, where she blindly celebrated a future that would never come; in the Palm Court tea parlor where she realized her lover's heartbreaking deceit; on the top floor where she searched, panic-stricken, for the door out of the building; and finally, on the roof itself, where she almost found the strength to go on.

Curiously, no one has ever reported a run-in with the Woman in Red on the sidewalk where she actually met her end. Rather, she is encountered at the locations where her emotions ran strongest in the hour before death. Seasoned ghost hunters will not be surprised, as true hauntings are believed to be *residual;* that is, there are no actual spirits present. Rather, the *energy* of the traumatic event creates an imprint on the location, like a video that may be viewed over and over, sometimes for centuries. Such was likely the case with the "ghost" of Ruth Steinhagen at the Edgewater Beach, and such may be the case of the "ghost" of the Woman in Red.

Infestation: The Congress Plaza

One of Chicago's largest hotels, the Congress Plaza, was originally named the Auditorium Annex when it was built to house visitors to the Columbian Exposition—the transformative World's Fair of 1893. The name referenced the Auditorium Theater across Congress Street, an acoustically magnificent structure designed by blockbuster architectural duo Dankmar Adler and

Louis Sullivan. The Annex's original North Tower was designed by Clinton Warren, but Adler and Sullivan oversaw its development, including the addition of "Peacock Alley," an ornate marble tunnel which ran under the street joining the theater and the hotel. Later, in the early-twentieth century, the firm of Holabird and Roche designed the South Tower, completing the current structure which houses more than eight hundred rooms.

The South Tower construction included a magnificent banquet hall, now known as the Gold Room, which would become the first hotel ballroom in America to use air-conditioning. Another ballroom, called the Florentine Room, was added to the North Tower in 1909. These two famous public rooms combined with the Elizabethan Room and the Pompeian Room to host Chicago's elite social events of the day.

On June 15, 2003, members of the Unite Here Local 1 on staff at the Congress began a strike after the hotel froze employee wages and revoked key benefits, including health insurance and retirement plans. Through the long months and years, the strikers have won countless supporters, their cause garnering momentum around the world. Even future president Barack Obama and Illinois Governor Patrick Quinn have walked their picket line, while the skeleton crew that continues to punch the clock is reported to pocket wages of more than thirty percent below the national standard. As of this writing, more than six years after it began, the Congress Hotel strike claims the unfortunate honor as the longest hotel strike in history, leaving in its wake a hotel haunted by pulled proms, boycotted conventions, and an estimated loss of seven hundred million dollars in revenue.

And many, many ghosts.

Indeed, the ghosts of the Congress are everywhere—and no wonder. Grover Cleveland, William McKinley, Teddy Roosevelt, William Howard Taft, Woodrow Wilson, Warren Harding, Calvin Coolidge, and Franklin Roosevelt all made the Congress their base of operations while in Chicago, leading to the hotel's longtime moniker, "The Home of Presidents." In 1912, President

Theodore Roosevelt announced his new "Bull Moose" platform in the Florentine Ballroom, and in 1932 the hotel served as headquarters for Franklin Roosevelt and his hopeful Democratic Party. A few years later, Benny Goodman broadcast his wildly popular radio show from the hotel's Urban Room, a posh nightclub that drew the city's most coveted clientele, and in 1971, President Richard Nixon addressed the Midwest Chapters of the AARP and National Retired Teachers Association, speaking before no less than three thousand members and guests in the hotel's Great Hall. For years, Al Capone played cards every Friday night in one of the hotel's meeting rooms, and rumors abound (though most certainly false) that he even owned the Congress for awhile. What *is* true is that Jake "Greasy Thumb" Guzik phoned Capone in Palm Island, Florida, from a phone in the Congress Plaza... before and after the St. Valentine's Day Massacre.

But the ghosts of the Congress are not those of headline-grabbers. Rather, they are wisps of memory, glimmers of the hundreds of thousands of ordinary guests who have glided through its halls for more than a century.

The Florentine Room, an ornately painted ballroom, was originally a roller rink. Security guards say that, on their wee-hour rounds, cheerful organ music can still be heard from outside the locked doors, as well as the sound of old wooden skate wheels against the wooden floors.

In the lavish Gold Room, a hotspot for Chicago wedding receptions, brides and grooms are often chilled by photographer's photos. Those snapped around the grand piano tend to develop with one or more people missing from the pictures.

In the South Tower, the third floor hallways are home to a one-legged man, often reported to the front desk by guests who think a vagrant has found his way inside, and in the hotel lobby a boy in knickers is often seen hiding behind the columns.

Only one guest room in the South Tower is reported to be haunted, room 905, where constant phone static has bedeviled guests for years.

Photograph courtesy of Michael Spudic

Was the Congress Hotel the inspiration for Stephen King's *1408*?

But the North Tower? That's a different story.

There is the phantom who lingers at the fifth floor passenger elevator, where moaning is often heard by guests awaiting its arrival. In room 474 a once-resident judge eternally changes the channels on his cherished television set. In room 759 another erstwhile resident pulls the door shut from inside when guests try to enter. It is said that he was an elderly gentleman—a longtime resident—whose son had come to take him to a nursing home many years ago. Wanting to stay put at the hotel, he mustered the strength to try to keep his son (and security guards) from opening the door. Even now he remains, determined to live at the Congress forever.

And then there are the rooms that no one will number: the room where the pictures on the wall rotate 360 degrees before the eyes of astonished borders; the room where an impromptu exorcism was allegedly held on some unidentified Chicago winter's night not so long ago; the room fled by two Marines, running through the lobby in their boxer shorts at 3:00 A.M., with the later explanation that a towering black figure had entered the room from the closet and approached their beds.

And then there is THE room.

Researchers have come to believe that it was a room here at the Congress Plaza that partly inspired writer Stephen King to create his short story, *1408,* a gripping tale of a professional—and skeptical—ghost hunter who meets his match in a mysterious hotel room (1408) said to be too haunted to lease. Unbelieving, the young man convinces the hotel's manager to let him have the room for a night, though the previous tenants all took their own lives during their stays in it. The real-life 1408 is believed to remain today on the Congress's most haunted floor, the twelfth floor of the older North Tower. There is no number anymore; in fact, there is no door anymore. The room has been walled up and papered over, though the old door frame remains.

IV.

Deliver Us

From ghoulies and ghosties
Long-leggedy beasties
And things that go bump in the night,
Good Lord, deliver us.

—Scottish prayer

*C*hicago's folklore belies a strongly religious base. Many of Chicago's greatest ghost stories are those of hauntings stemming from sacred sources, including the tale of the dreaded Devil Baby of Hull-House, a nasty infant born to an atheistic father who chastised his pregnant wife for her Catholic faith. Appropriately, many of Chicago's churches have haunting tales to tell. *Chicago Haunts* passed on the story of Father Arnold Damen, founder of Holy Family Church, one of the oldest in Chicago, believed to still watch over his beloved congregation.

The lingering tale of St. Michael's Church in Old Town is one that's hard to shake. Decades ago, a hooded, cloven-hooved figure was reportedly seen in the Communion line at Mass by scores of parishioners before vanishing into thin air.

St. Rita's Church on Chicago's South Side, old timers still talk about that All Souls' Day in the early 1960s when a group of devotees literally fled the church after sighting a host of hooded phantoms in the choir loft.

But stories of church hauntings continue to surface.

St. Charles Borromeo stood near Roosevelt Road and Damen Avenue until its demolition in the late 1960s. Though the church itself boasted no ghost stories that still circulate, the haunting of its rectory has become immortalized by Rocco Facchini's popular book, *Muldoon: A True Chicago Ghost Story*. Rocco was a freshly-ordained priest in the 1950s; his first assignment was St. Charles, where he was disappointed to find—in an age of highly-staffed parishes, bustling rectories, and priestly communality—only the pastor as the other priest on staff and, literally, a handful of parishioners remaining after decades of the neighborhood's drastic socio-economic change. Rocco soon discovered that the rectory was haunted by more than the ghost of its former prosperity; it was quite literally haunted by the specter of the parish's founder, Bishop Peter Muldoon.

As his months at St. Charles played out, Rocco was astonished to find that the pastor himself lived in mortal terror of Muldoon's ghost, locking himself in his room each night because Muldoon was "out to get him," presumably because the pastor had lost his faith—and his love of the parish and congregation. Today, unfortunately, those looking for the old rectory will be disappointed to find in its stead the parking garage for the Cook County Juvenile Court; the church and its accompanying buildings were torn down in 1968.

◆

At St. Margaret Mary Parish on the Northwest Side, ghostly rumors still circulate of a most unusual variety. The story dates to the 1960s when one of the priests or perhaps the monsignor on staff at the church kept a pet brown bear. After years of living as an honorary parishioner, the bear eventually died, but parishioners claim the bear can still be seen sometimes, especially near the old incinerator, where it liked to linger while alive. Sometimes, on winter evenings, they say you can still hear its low growl.

◆

Visitation Church, on West Garfield Boulevard, is home to the "Phantom Midnight Mass," which was reported from time to time by parishioners passing the church at night in the days when the doors were always open. According to stories still told by old-timers, an occasional witness would be passing at midnight or later through the darkened neighborhood and hear a voice resounding beyond the church walls. Curious, the passer-by would crack open the vestibule door to find an astonishing sight:

an unfamiliar priest in full liturgical dress celebrating the Mass with not a congregant in sight. According to parishioners, this was believed to be the specter of a priest who had died without celebrating a memorial Mass for one of the faithful departed.

◆

Not too long ago, a former altar server at St. Patricia Church in Hickory Hills—now a grown woman—told me about an experience she'd had during her days attending the parish school:

> On a weekday morning in 1995, I was doing my duty as altar server for the morning weekday Mass at St. Patricia. I was only in seventh grade at the time and was sitting on the altar. This church is a little older and has one aisle, orange-brown carpet with dark brown pews, stained glass windows, and different shades of orange paint behind the altar. This is the school I attended from first through eighth grade. My whole life I have been open to different occurrences but had never witnessed anything personally.
>
> The Mass was not full by any means because it was a weekday morning. Many pews were empty and the priest was giving his Homily. As I looked around I noticed something under one of the pews. Of course, I did a double take and rubbed my eyes to make sure it was not just my imagination. Under one of the pews on the left side (from my point of view) near the front and center were two heads. One was of an older woman and the other of a young boy. They were laughing and looked as if they were playing. Again I tried to look around and rub my eyes, but they were still there. They were harmless and did not do anything besides laugh and play. I only ever saw their heads, but the details of their faces and their actions were quite clear. Afraid to tell anyone during school what I had

seen, I waited until I was at home and told my mom. She encouraged me to believe what I saw to be real and also pointed out who they might be.

Within the parish there had been a little Boy Scout who had passed away, and there was a flag/memorial put up for him next to the church. Also, there was a teacher who had died that worked at the school. I believe these two faces where those two people. I never knew either of these two people when they were alive, but I feel I was able to see them because I was at an age when we are more open to these occurrences. I do not really know why I saw them, but I do know I have full belief that it can happen and does; we are just too busy or jaded to recognize what is going on around us. Now that I am older I am more convicted in what I saw and that it was real.

◆

For me, of course, the most fascinating ghost stories of all are those of St. Benedict Church, at Irving Park Road and Leavitt Street, where I grew up. I was baptized and confirmed at St. Benedict, received my First Eucharist there, and was married there in 1998, amid scaffolding and wet plaster while the church was undergoing a complete restoration to prepare for the new millennium. I was privileged to be sent through twelve years of school there, and I—with my young daughters—still attend Sunday Mass at the parish and sing in the choir.

The family environment at St. Benedict grew from its founding in 1902, stemming from the desire of local families for a nearby Catholic school. At the time, West Lakeview-area Catholics attended St. Matthias Parish (now the combined parishes of St. Matthias/Transfiguration), at Western Avenue and Ainslie Street. Children of the current St. Benedict area were pressed to make the long and sometimes dangerous walk to the school of St. Matthias, often crossing streets where trolley cars ran.

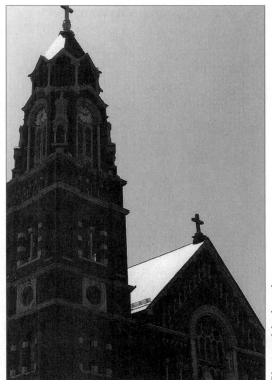

Photograph by the author

My beloved St. Benedict Church, on Iriving Park Road.

Unlike the massive, cathedral-like structure that stands to-day, the original building was a combination wooden church and school, quickly outgrown by a congregation that quadrupled between 1902 and 1908, fed largely by families migrating from the downtown church of St. Joseph's, the North Side's first German parish. A new church was built to meet the needs of the burgeoning parish—a brick structure at Irving Park and present-day Bell Avenue—which housed a church on the second floor and a school and meeting room on the first. This building—still used by the parish as a social hall and gymnasium—also quickly fell short of the needs of the community, and it was evident that bigger plans must be made for the future.

In 1918, the existing church was completed, built largely with donations from parish families at a cost of $170,000 and featuring stained-glass windows from Munich and hand-carved Stations of the Cross from Oberammergau.

It was during the construction of the present-day church that the ghost stories began. While working on the interior of the altar wall, a worker fell from the scaffolding and died on the altar floor. Over the years, the figure of a man in work clothes has been seen behind the columns that back the altar, and the sound of moaning or sobbing has been heard in the sacristy.

Over many years, choir members rehearsing in the church at night near the altar have reported seeing a figure sitting in the darkened pews, near the front, to the left of the aisle. When I was a girl, one of my best friend's brothers was a maintenance worker at the church. He claimed that each morning, when he opened the church for 6:30 Mass, he would hear the unmistakable sound of someone getting up from a kneeler and the kneeler banging closed. No one can guess if these sightings are related to the death during construction or if they are, more likely, the lingering of a faithful parishioner, keeping the night watch near the tabernacle.

One of the scarier stories I've heard about St. Benedict came from a friend of my late godmother's. My Aunt Frannie moved to the suburb of Brookfield about eight years before her death; until that time she grew up and stayed living in my grandmother's house, just a block or so from church. Each morning she would attend the 6:30 Mass with a number of other older women and men of the parish. Before Mass, a few ultra-early birds would gather to pray the Rosary until Mass began. There was a woman named Dora who was one of these, and one morning, sometime in the early 1990s, she arrived before anyone else, going to her usual pew on the main aisle and kneeling down to pray. After a few moments, she heard the heavy, rear outer door open and bang shut and the soft whoosh of the interior door. Measured footsteps started up the aisle as Dora continued to pray, expecting one of the gentlemen of the morning group to pass her and sit in his usual pew a few rows ahead. When the footsteps reached a point just over her shoulder; however, they suddenly stopped. Wondering why, Dora turned and saw not any of the morning regulars but a tall, pale man dressed in black with a black English-style bowler hat on his head.

Dora was a meek woman, and she was startled by the presence of this stranger in the empty church, but before she could make a move or say a word, he threw his head back and laughed a shrill, almost cartoon-like laugh. Dora was petrified, paralyzed. The man looked down at the Rosary in her hands and then into her eyes. "You know that won't help you," he said. Then he turned to walk back down the aisle as he came, but as she stared, frozen, Dora saw that the man had hooves where his feet should have been.

V.

Watery Graves

They might have split up or they might have capsized
They may have broke deep and took water
And all that remains is the faces and the names
Of the wives and the sons and the daughters.

—Gordon Lightfoot
"The Wreck of the Edmund Fitzgerald"

C hicago Haunts and *More Chicago Haunts* both explored the ghosts of Chicago's beloved Lake Michigan shoreline, from the North Shore specter of "Seaweed Charlie" to the South Shore apparition of the fabled Diana of the Dunes, but the stories of this city's haunted waters are as endless as the view across the lake on a summer afternoon.

Water is often closely associated with haunting experiences and legends. In Chicago, the watery hosts: Lake Michigan, the Chicago, Des Plaines and Fox Rivers, the Illinois and Michigan Canal—and the areas surrounding them—all harbor their own resident phantoms. At least two theories suggest the reason. Either ghosts are unable to cross water, and so they "build up" along the shores of lakes, rivers, and other bodies of water. Or, ghosts love water, because it's a great conductor for their electrical energies.

According to the first theory, Chicago residents through the Edwardian era often followed the ancient custom of keeping pails of water on the attic and basement stairs so that the ghosts in these areas would be unable to access the occupied areas of the house.

To understand the second theory, realize that most ghosts that are seen inside are seen in the bathroom. Researchers have come to wonder if water—especially running water—gives ghosts a way to "conduct" their own energies, to manifest themselves more easily and efficiently.

Whatever the reason, a number of water ghosts have become much enmeshed in local folklore. Sometimes, the rumors of them

Photograph by the author

**Waterfront highrises on Lake Shore Drive,
with some terrifying tenants.**

betray shocking realities—and, just maybe, some interesting possibilities.

And the stories keep coming.

A few months ago I was contacted by a woman who had
attended school at St. Mary of the Lake on Sheridan Road, just
a few blocks from Lake Michigan. While in eighth grade, on All
Souls' Day of 1960, she had a most unusual experience at Cricket
Hill, a grassy toboggan slope with a beautiful view of the water:

> *Since (it) was a Holy Day, we were out of school. My
> friend and I, along with her aunt and mother decided to
> walk to the park (Clarendon Park) which was only a couple
> blocks east. As we were walking the path, my friend and
> I... started running toward Cricket Hill, and as we ap-*

*proached we saw "hooded monks" going up the side of
the hill (north to south). As we continued we noticed how
they seemed to glide. The first one had reached the top
and the rest followed, gliding on air. Of course it scared
the —— out of us, and we ran back toward her mom and
aunt. As we reached them, they too had noticed that they
could see clearly from the ground to the end of their robes.
I remember they had the hoods up and appeared to have
their hands folded in prayer.*

The Lake Michigan Triangle

The first mention of strange goings-on in the so-called "Bermuda Triangle" were by Christopher Columbus, who claimed to have experienced a number of the phenomena that would be encountered by Triangle victims in later centuries. Notably, Columbus wrote that the crew had spotted bizarre sea animals and mysterious lights along the Triangle area, hundreds of years before its christening, and reported that, while in the Triangle area, malfunctioning instruments had left them directionless more than once. The modern recognition of the area as "mysterious" first came in 1951, when reporter E.V.W. Jones coined the term "The Devil's Triangle" in an Associated Press report on the disappearances of planes and boats in the area. Over many decades, scores of seacraft and aircraft have vanished from the Triangle, sometimes moments after signaling for mooring or landing.

The Great Lakes have long been known for their own "Triangle-esque" phenomena. Though together known as The Great Lakes Triangle, each of the lakes has its own treacherous, anomalous sector. In Chicago, sailors and pilots are well aware of the dangers of our Lake Michigan Triangle.

The boundaries of the Lake Michigan Triangle run through the lake from the ferry town of Ludington, Michigan, southward to Benton Harbor, Michigan, and from Benton Harbor to the Wisconsin town of Manitowoc, which connects by ferry back across the lake to Ludington. Our own Triangle, like the Bermuda Triangle, is notorious for its mysterious fogs, instrumental disturbances, and ghost ships and planes.

In May 2000, in fact, the problem of ghost planes turning up on radar was covered by no less than the *Chicago Sun-Times*, which interviewed officers of the local controllers union who claimed the FAA was not being honest about the magnitude of the recent issue. At the time, the FAA admitted there had been 'Thirteen ghost images in the last five weeks rather than the usual eight or nine the FAA would normally expect in this time period.' Union officers claimed it was closer to 130.

The next year in early December 2001, a tiny Cessna plane—carrying no less than three licensed pilots with more than fifty years experience among them—disappeared over the Triangle while making a leisurely trip from Dayton, Ohio, to Racine, Wisconsin. The Milwaukee Coast Guard assumed the single-engine craft had met its fate by sinking into the lake near Wilmette Harbor, just north of Chicago, but no sign of the craft or the passengers was found.

At the time of the disappearance, older pilots in the area remembered a bizarre incident that had occurred in the summer of 1950, when a commercial airliner left New York for Minneapolis, never to be seen again. Northwestern Airlines flight 2501 would reach the skies above Battle Creek, Michigan, just before midnight before changing course to avoid weather problems in Chicago. Rerouting took the DC-4 over Lake Michigan waters, but as the plane headed northwest towards the Wisconsin border, it simply vanished, and no trace of it would ever be found.

Disappearances in the Lake Michigan Triangle occur on the water as well. One of the most puzzling of such cases remains an incident concerning the freighter *O.M. McFarland;* specifically, its captain, George R. Donner, who vanished from his cabin in April 1937, during a haul through the Great Lakes from Erie, Pennsylvania, to Port Washington, Wisconsin.

Because it was only early spring, sheets of ice still glazed much of the upper lakes, and Captain Donner stood watch for seemingly endless hours snaking a breathtaking path through the dangerous waters. When the *McFarland* reached Lake Michigan, crew and captain breathed a sigh of relief and prepared for an easy last leg of the voyage.

Captain Donner went below to rest before reaching Port Washington, but when the second mate went to rouse him as the ship neared port, Donner could not be awakened. Pounding on the locked cabin door brought no response, so the crew eventually forced it open, finding the room empty. All hands searched the ship—in vain. No trace of Donner was ever found, though it was duly noted that the *McFarland* was sailing through the Lake Michigan Triangle when the incident occurred.

Kathy Doore is a veteran sailor who has spent many hours on the Great Lakes, many of them engaged in the races that draw thousands of participants each season. It was during a practice sail in preparation for one such race that Doore had what she still calls her "Lake Michigan Triangle" experience. Her truly haunting recollection of that night perfectly captures the physicality and emotionality of the Triangle's spell:

> *July 1978, a perfect night for a sail with seven to ten knot winds, flat seas, and, as it was mid-week, we had the lake to ourselves. I was aboard one of three classic wooden sailboats, part of an active racing fleet that competed every Sunday and practiced several times a week. Around dusk on this sultry July evening, we set sail for what should have been an idyllic cruise; as fate would have it, the gods had something different in mind.*

> *Not an hour out of port, and quite unexpectedly, a dense fog rapidly descended upon us. Visibility dropped to zero. We became disoriented and feared we'd crash into one another. The winds were erratic, filling the mainsail from two opposing directions, a phenomenon no one*

had ever experienced before this evening. Suddenly, I was extremely cold. In fact, I was freezing.

I turned to ask my crewmates if they were cold, and to my utter astonishment, they were no longer standing next to me! One moment we had been packed into the tiny cockpit like sardines, and the very next instant, I was alone at the helm. Dumfounded, I called out and located them on the back deck, where it was several degrees warmer. They seemed perplexed, and urged me to join them. That's when I noticed that no one was steering the boat.

The captain raised his arms high over his head, glee-fully wiggling his hands and fingers in the air, and stated he hadn't been steering for the past ten minutes. Yet not a minute before, I was certain he had been standing behind me at the helm. Draped in dense fog, the vessel began a curious, aquatic dance. Slowly, but deliberately, she turned on her axis, completing three perfect, 360-degree pirouettes, never crossing the wind. Then, just as suddenly as it had appeared, the fog dissipated. To our utter astonishment, we saw the other two boats pirouetting in exactly the same manner. A moment later, we regained control of the vessel and pulled out of the vortex. In unison, all three boats turned and headed for port.

Sailing home over a placid, glass-like sea beneath the newly-risen full moon, I found myself enfolded in the tangible presence of my recently-deceased father. My crewmates, also, seemed lost in some kind of inexplicable rapture; the only sound was an occasional splash on the rail.

We noticed the lead boat enter the anchorage; it had once belonged to our captain, and we knew it well. As we approached the tiny inlet, we found our old mooring empty, the sister ship nowhere in sight. All was quiet. We scanned the horizon for mast movement. We were the only vessel underway.

We couldn't imagine where the other boat could have gone. In fact, there was no place they could go. We set out in search of them but to no avail. A few minutes later, we circled back and were astonished to see that they were not only tied up with sails stowed but were rowing ashore. Nothing added up. Time either stood still or sped up.

After the third boat arrived, we met onshore. This usually boisterous group seemed dazed and wanted nothing more than to go home and go to sleep. It seemed we'd been out for no more than two or perhaps three hours instead of six. It was now well past midnight. As the weeks passed, I realized we couldn't account for a good portion of that evening.

The following Sunday, as we readied ourselves for the big race, I brought up the unusual events from our extraordinary sail. To my utter astonishment, no one would talk about it. Worse yet, they behaved as if nothing out of the ordinary had happened! The vortical winds alone would have given them fodder for years. It became evident that I was the only one in remembrance.

I asked Kathy Doore what she felt when she looked back, now, on the incident that occurred nearly thirty years ago. In retrospect, what happened? Like many witnesses of the various Triangle phenomena—both here in the Great Lakes and in the infamous Bermuda area—Doore believes she and the crew

had temporarily entered a 'parallel reality' from the moment I looked down into the water and called out to my crewmates until we entered port and found the other crew rowing ashore, re-emerging into the present timeline.

Photograph by the author

A view of the lake from the bird sanctuary at Montrose Point.

Ghost Ships of Lake Michigan

Ghost ships have been sighted throughout sailing history, and many famous phantom vessels still traverse waters around the world, including the matchless *Flying Dutchman,* most often sighted near South Africa's Cape of Good Hope. Though the *Dutchman* has no known historical origins, glimpses of the ship have been reported through the ages. Most legends call the *Dutchman* diabolical, likely stemming from the rumor that its true captain was in league with the devil. Sailing superstition dreads a run-in with the fearsome vessel; an encounter is believed to be a portent of death.

One of the most famous and reliable sightings of the *Dutchman* was that of King George V in 1881 while he sailed on the HMS *Bacchante.* Near the coast of Australia, the future king wrote:

At 4 A.M. the Flying Dutchman *crossed our bows. A strange red light as of a phantom ship all aglow, in the midst of which light the masts, spars, and sails of a brig*

*two hundred yards distant stood out in strong relief as
she came up on the port bow, where also the officer of the
watch from the bridge clearly saw her, as did the quar-
terdeck midshipman, who was sent forward at once to the
forecastle; but on arriving there was no vestige nor any
sign whatever of any material ship was to be seen either
near or right away to the horizon, the night being clear
and the sea calm.*

Later that morning, at just after ten, the deckhand who had
first glimpsed the *Dutchman* died in a freak accident on board the
Bacchante.

♦

Of course, on the Great Lakes, no ghost ship can match
that of the ill-fated *Edmund Fitzgerald*, a lake freighter that
sank on Lake Superior during a notorious gale on November 10,
1975, without so much as a distress signal. When a search and
rescue party reached the scene, debris from the *Fitz* was found,
but the crew had seemingly vanished into thin air. Though later
investigations drew sensible and probable conclusions about the
demise of the *Fitzgerald* and its crew, the initial enigma of its fall
led the ship into infamy, where it remains shrouded in mystery.
Adding to the ambiguity of the *Fitz's* fate are numerous reports of
its ghostly counterpart, said to yet sail the gale-tossed waters of
Lake Superior. But, on the Great Lakes, the *Fitzgerald* does not
sail alone. Lake Michigan has at least two ghost ships of its own.

In early September 1860, the steamer *Lady Elgin* headed
out of the port of Milwaukee bound for Chicago. Most of the
passengers were members of Wisconsin's Union Guard, traveling
to Chicago for a campaign rally featuring presidential hopeful
Stephen Douglas. Though foul weather was forecasted, the short
trip to Chicago passed without incident. On the return trip that
same evening, however, just before midnight a fierce gale erupted,
causing a nearby, diminutive schooner, the *Augusta,* to approach

the *Lady Elgin* for assistance. Out of control, the *Augusta* collided with the steamer, driving a hole into the port side and causing all of *Lady Elgin*'s lights to fail.

Terrified, the crew of the *Augusta* headed for the safety of Chicago, not realizing the damage that the *Lady Elgin* had suffered. On that steamboat, all hands rushed to throw cargo overboard to raise the gash above water level. Even live cattle were hurled into the lake in a panicked effort to save the ship and its passengers, the latter bound to the vessel—for better or worse—when the *Elgin's* lifeboat drifted away.

Shockingly, within a half hour, the *Lady Elgin* had sunk. Shortly thereafter, the sun rose on hundreds of bodies in the freezing water—many, many dead, some fighting for life. In the end, more than four hundred death certificates were issued to victims who either drowned in the wreck or died from being tossed against the rocky shoreline. The loss of the *Lady Elgin* would remain the second-deadliest disaster in Great Lakes history, second only to the horrific *Eastland* Disaster, which took more than 840 lives in 1915 on the Chicago River—in nineteen feet of water.

According to sailors, the *Lady Elgin* has sailed Lake Michigan each anniversary night since its demise. Though the ship is silent, her passengers are not. In fact, seamen have long told tales of picking up castaways from the autumn waters who claim to have abandoned a steamboat *en route* to Milwaukee. While crews search vainly for the distressed vessel, the rescued passengers vanish without a trace, further panicking the bewildered rescuers.

Strollers along the North Shore, too, have told of similar encounters with wild-eyed stragglers who have literally walked out of the lake in the wee hours, soaking wet and begging for help for their distraught vessel. Interestingly, passengers of the *Elgin* who made it to shore had, in fact, been aided by just such strollers—predominantly students from the lakeshore campus of Northwestern University—whose efforts inspired the founding of the university's student-run U.S. Life Saving Station in 1876, the first installation of federal life saving resources on the Great Lakes, which has since orchestrated more than five hundred rescues.

♦

In November 1912, the same year as the *Titanic* Disaster, Lake Michigan bore witness to its own maritime mishap when the schooner *Rouse Simmons* disappeared, believed to have gone down in a violent storm somewhere between southern Wisconsin and Chicago. Due to a lack of physical evidence and credible witness reports, no one knows for sure what fate befell the craft.

The three-masted *Rouse Simmons* was not just an ordinary Great Lakes sailing ship. Rather, it was known affectionately as the "Christmas Tree Ship" or the "Santa Claus Ship." The cargo it off-loaded annually at the Clark Street docks of the Chicago River included thousands of pine and evergreen trees from Michigan's north woods that Chicagoans purchased and decorated as Christmas trees.

Various reports from the time say Captain Herman Schuenemann, his wife, and a crew of sixteen men left port near Manistique, Michigan, on the afternoon of November 25, 1912, bound for Chicago with an estimated arrival date two days later.

In his 1977 volume, *The Great Lakes Triangle*, author Jay Gourley writes that the *Rouse Simmons* was spotted off the shore of Sturgeon Bay, Wisconsin, by observers manning the United States Life Saving Station there. The ship was reportedly flying distress signals, but because of the vessel's rapid speed, the men at the station didn't attempt to launch a rescue vessel for fear they wouldn't be able to catch her. Instead, a message was sent to the next station twenty-five miles south. There rescuers headed into the lake in a large surfboat in an attempt to reach the *Rouse Simmons*. Reports say the *Rouse Simmons* was seen in the water but that a mysterious veil of heavy mist suddenly enveloped the schooner, causing it to disappear from sight forever. When the fog lifted, the *Rouse Simmons* was gone. A week later, a haunting load of evergreen wreaths and Christmas trees washed ashore at Pentwater, Michigan, but no sign of the ship or her crew was found for nearly a century, save for Schuenemann's wallet, pulled from the lake by commercial fishermen ten years later during a harvest of salmon.

Over the years, various theories have emerged regarding the ship's fate, though none have been confirmed because the *Rouse Simmons* left almost no credible or verifiable evidence of its disappearance. One exception was reported in the *Chicago Tribune* eight months after the *Rouse Simmons'* disappearance, which wrote of a young boy playing on a stretch of Lake Michigan beach near Sturgeon Bay, Wisconsin, who discovered a note that had washed ashore in a bottle. The note was written by Captain Charles Nelson, Captain Schuenemann's partner on the *Rouse Simmons*. The dispatch read as follows, "These lines are written at 10:30 P.M. Schooner *Rouse Simmons* ready to go down... between fifteen and twenty miles off shore. All hands lashed to one line. Good-bye. Capt. Charles Nelson."

Today, nearly a century after its disappearance, the fate of the *Rouse Simmons* remains elusive and speculative. Newspaper reports at the time wondered if the ship had lost its seaworthiness due to decay and lack of maintenance. Other opinions ventured that a tremendous gale from a Great Lakes storm simply blew over the water and caused the schooner to sink to the bottom. No bodies or wreckage were ever recovered. Even modern day diving expeditions over the years have failed to uncover a single scrap of the missing ship or one bone of a lone passenger.

Yet, for several years after the ship's disappearance, reports published in local newspapers told of unexplained sightings of a phantom or ghost ship fitting the exact description of the *Rouse Simmons* sailing on Lake Michigan, her sails in tatters. To this day it is said that, toward November's end, one can still catch the scent of Christmas trees wafting on the air along the Lake Michigan shoreline or near the site of the old Clark Street dock once used by the merry vessel.

Finally, in 1971 the wreck of the *Rouse Simmons* was discovered by Milwaukee diver Gordon Kent Bellrichard during his search for another missing ship, the *Vernon*, a steamer that had disappeared in 1887. One hundred and seventy feet below the surface, the *Simmons* slumbered. Amazingly, most of the Christmas trees were still on board.

A number of artifacts from the *Simmons* are on permanent display, including two of the trees and the ship's wheel. The anchor of the ship was installed at the entrance of the Milwaukee Yacht Club.

Mile away, a more elusive souvenir survives. In Norridge's Acacia Park Cemetery, just west of Chicago, the grave of Captain Schuenemann's wife is reported to be alive with a curious phenomenon. Though the cemetery grass is close-cropped and bare of trees, Schuenemann's grave, they say, is ever blanketed by a festive and evocative smell: the unmistakable scent of pine needles.

Tales from the Riverbank

Lake Michigan is certainly a force to be reckoned with, but other sites in Chicago have earned their reputations as dangerous waters, most notably the Fox River.

The town of Yorkville has witnessed some of the most publicized drownings along the often-dangerous Fox. The problem areas of this beautiful natural resource are the dams that dot it. Dams are problematic for humans because swimmers and recreational boaters can be sucked into the boil of the falling waters and trapped by the undercurrent. At the controversial Glen Palmer Dam in Yorkville, no less than seventeen deaths have occurred as of this writing since its construction in 1960, including those of three men in late spring of 2006, one a Villa Park resident whose kayak fell prey to the dam's force—and two brothers who tried to save him.

Resulting from these tragedies has been a growing outrage about the dam's continued existence and, in 2006, an authorization by the Illinois governor to rebuild it. Family members of victims, horrified area residents, and Friends of the Fox River—who criticize the environmental fallout of dams in general—mounted a campaign to stop the rebuilding of the dam and remove it altogether. Champions of the dam rebuilding dismissed such concerns, ignoring the environmental issues and claiming that the new stepped design planned for the dam would remove most of the safety issues involved.

Is this why, in the wee hours of random Sunday mornings, witnesses continue to sight some of the victims of the Glen Palmer Dam in ghostly form? Indeed, many have seen the family of distressed canoers trying to make their way through the waters from the dam to riverfront area and disappearing *en route*. Most report that there are three apparitions: a man holding a single canoe paddle, a young girl with a life jacket in hand, and a woman who appears to be crying. Some believe that this is the family of a five-year-old girl said to have drowned at the dam and that this apparition is not a ghostly one but a true haunting, a permanent impression on the landscape created, perhaps, by the devastating emotions of the family at the time of the drowning and, just maybe, fueled by the ongoing fears of the living.

Creatures from the Black Lagoon?

Great Lakes and dam-studded rivers are terrifying owing to their sheer force and unpredictability, but in Chicago and elsewhere, placid bodies can equally chill—not because of natural forces but human nature.

In the city, every drop of the Jackson Park Lagoon delights ghost-lovers. Glistening along Chicago's South Shore, the lagoon lies behind the Museum of Science and Industry, one of the only remaining structures from city planner Daniel Burnham's magical *White City* of the 1893 Columbian Exposition. Steps lead from the rear portico to the water, and *Chicago Haunts* readers will remember that these steps are still frequented by the late Clarence Darrow. Darrow—Chicago's matchless criminal defender who prominently figured in the so-called Scopes Monkey Trial and the Trial of the Century (the Chicago case of Leopold and Loeb)—requested that his ashes be scattered over the lagoon he loved. Friends and

Photograph by the author

Looking across the Jackson Park Lagoon from the Wooded Island, toward the Museum of Science and Industry.

strangers, sure enough, have seen him standing on those rear steps, gazing over the waters of his final resting place.

Today, Jackson Park and its lagoon are frequented by families of the nearby Englewood neighborhood, one of the city's poorest, and it is the children of Englewood who tell the most frightening tales of the park's ghostly waters. According to them, each year on Halloween night a horrifying event occurs—the ghostly victims of all those murdered in Englewood since the last All Hallows' Eve rise up out of the Jackson Park Lagoon to seek revenge on their killers. These ghouls have from midnight to dawn to accomplish the task, for when the sun breaks over Lake Michigan, they must return to their graves, with or without their prey.

If you think you can escape the horrors of Jackson Park by taking cover inside the Museum of Science and Industry, think again. Inside the Museum, the ghost of serial murderer H.H. Holmes (of *Devil in the White City* fame) stalks invisible victims in the cobblestoned Yesterday's Main Street exhibit, while phantom passengers lounge aboard the now-stationary, streamlined Burlington Zephyr train, a sleek, deco-era beauty which once rocketed through Chicago to the delight of the city's children, who made nightly treks to the tracks to wait for the Silver Streak's breathtaking passage. No story in the museum is more notorious, however, than another watery tale, the haunting of the *U-505* submarine.

The *U-505*

The *U-505* was one of the terrifying German submarines (or U-boats) that ruled the seas during the early years of World War II. U-boats actually cruised the seas above the waterline, stalking merchant ships. Only after a sighting would the U-boat captain order submersion, in order to approach with stealth aided by periscope. Once the U-boat got close enough to attack, a torpedo was launched to sink the merchant ship by blasting a whole in its hull.

After their introduction, U-boat attacks on merchant ships soon numbered in the hundreds, causing merchant crews to dread travel on the open seas. Allied merchant ships began to travel in convoys of up to two hundred vessels for protection, but a U-boat attack still called off all bets, disrupting a convoy's formation and undermining the safety of all members. Often, the convoys were escorted by powerful destroyers that would launch depth charges in response to U-boat offensives, but fear still reigned, as many deaths typically occurred during these exchanges.

Furthering the fear was Adolph Hitler's response to the convoys, his own fleets of U-boats—the so-called Wolfpacks—sent to pummel the Allied convoys. In the worst scenario of the competition, March 1943 brought an attack by more than three dozen U-boats on more than a hundred Allied craft, resulting in the sinking of a fifth of the Allied vessels.

By the time of this attack, the American navy had had enough. As assaults increased, the Allies took action, forming the Hunter-Killer Task Groups to hunt and destroy the U-boats, ship by ship. The task groups restored a great deal of peace to the minds of Allied seamen, and their formation increased as the war progressed, aided by advances in anti-sub intelligence

One of the most effective Hunter-Killer Task Groups was 22.3, whose escorts included the aircraft carrier USS *Guadalcanal*, home base for fighter planes whose pilots spent their days at sea monitoring the waters for U-boats and alerting 22.3's four destroyer escorts of the subs' positions.

Commander of the *Guadalcanal* was Chicago native Captain Daniel V. Gallery, Jr., a decorated pilot whose elegant and forceful direction in an earlier task group had led to the sinking of the *U-544*, the *U-68* and the *U-515*. While the sinking of the earlier U-boats had been a boon to the United States Navy and the Allies, Gallery had other plans for the new task group: capture an enemy sub.

If the navy were able to do it, such a capture would put into Allied hands priceless intelligence, including U-boat ammunition technology, insight into the Axis code system, ENIGMA, and precious communication logs. When the *Guadalcanal* set sail in the spring of 1944, capture was the mission.

The Tenth Fleet was the American antisubmarine intelligence command, headed up by Kenneth Knowles, and Gallery was debriefed by Knowles himself before setting out with Task Group 22.3. Knowles put Gallery and his group on the trail of a U-boat that had cast off two months earlier from France, headed toward the coast of Africa.

Task Group 22.3 bore for the Canary Islands on May 15, 1944, where Wildcat pilots joined the sea vessels in the hunt for the elusive sub. For nearly three weeks, search efforts dragged on, seemingly in vain; then, just as the search was abandoned, the destroyer USS *Chatelain* radioed sub contact... of the *U-505*.

Judging the sub's location, the *Chatelain* unleashed two dozen Mark 4 hedgehogs, missing the target. While the destroyer prepared for a second launch, *Guadalcanal* fighters tagged the sub's submerged location by firing rounds into the water. The *Chatelain* then fired more than a dozen Mark 9 depth charges—with success. Moments later, the sub burst to the surface.

Boarding the sub minutes later, the Allied boarding party worked against time to dismantle the scuttle charges, time bombs that would have been set by the crew during abandonment of the sub in order to sink the sub and prevent its capture. On the *U-505*, the crew had also tried to flood the ship by opening a pipe that allowed the inrush of water, but the boarding party was able to secure the opening and prevent further submersion of the craft.

While the boarding party carried out its dangerous work on the *U-505*, German sailors from the sub were rescued by Task Group 22.3 and taken prisoner aboard the *Guadalcanal* to await transport to a POW camp in Louisiana where they would remain until the end of hostilities.

Finally, the American crews prepared for the overwhelming task of towing the semi-submerged *U-505* to Bermuda—under United States Naval orders.

Though the sub eventually toured American cities as part of a bond drive, its days were numbered. After picking the sub apart for intelligence's sake, the U.S. Navy slated the sub to be employed in target practice, but retired Commander Daniel Gallery, as usual, had other plans.

Still moved by the import of the *U-505*—and his own experiences of its capture—Gallery sought the sub's survival and aimed to bring it to his own city of Chicago for permanent exhibition. Gallery found open ears to his plea at the Museum of Science and Industry, an astounding Chicago institution housed in one of the sprawling exhibit halls of the 1893 World's Fair. Then-president of the museum, Lenox Lohr, shared Gallery's hopes of acquiring a submarine for his inimitable museum, and he quickly approached U.S. Naval authorities with their desire for the *U-505*. The navy approved but would not front the monstrous expense of the actual transfer—a quarter of a million dollars.

Almost miraculously, the City of Chicago and the Museum of Science and Industry joined a slew of private organizations and individuals to raise the needed funds, and on May 15, 1954, exactly ten years after Task Group 22.3 had left port to find it, the

U-505 began the long tow from Portsmouth to Chicago, where it took more than a week to haul it out of Lake Michigan, across Lake Shore Drive, and across the museum's great front lawn of Jackson Park. That fall, the *U-505* became a memorial to the fallen of World War II; soon, it would obtain the status it retains as one of the museum's most popular exhibits.

When it was first installed as an exhibit, the *U-505's* home was actually outside the building, and visitors accessed the craft from an exhibit hall passageway inside the museum. Half a century of brutal, lakefront weather, however, took its toll, and in 1997, curators decided the sub would have to be moved indoors to remain safe for boarding.

After two years of repairing and refurbishing the *U-505* with the aid of antique photographs and eyewitness memories, the unthinkable task of moving the sub was again at hand. Luckily, experienced NORSAR signed on for the job, designing an elaborate system of dollies and jacks for the move into the museum and down into the *U-505*'s new, underground exhibit hall. But is all quiet on deck?

Nein.

Since its arrival at the museum, staff and visitors have been aware of an unseen sailor on the submarine. Surprisingly, the invisible crew member is not believed to be one of the vanquished of the infamous capture but former Commander Peter Zschech.

In October 1943, a year before its capture by Task Group 22.3, the *U-505* found itself enmeshed in battle with an Allied destroyer hailing from Britain, which attacked the sub with numerous depth charges. Believing his ship was near the end, Zschech took his own life, shooting himself in the head with his pistol as he stood, white-faced, at the controls. Even more horrifically, the shot hadn't instantly killed him, and as Zschech lay on his bunk, crying out, crew members muffled his cries with his pillow, to keep his voice from detection by the enemy and, as the men admitted, to quicken the inevitable end. Docents and security guards have both experienced unseen forces on the sub. In 2005, one security guard told of hearing voices on the *U-505* every single night she was on duty, and another reported sightings of a most unusual sort: the apparition of legs, feet, or shoes in the door of the commander's cabin, and the strong feeling of being watched while inside the room. Interestingly, in his autobiography, *U-505* submariner Hans Goebler writes that it was only when the crew saw the "lifeless legs" of Zschech being "dragged into the Olymp, our nickname for the area around the Skipper's cabin" that they "realized that something was very, very wrong."

Author and ghost hunter John Kachuba visited the museum before the move of the *U-505* and discovered that, while on the sub, one docent had felt an invisible presence attempt to enter his own body. Kachuba described his *U-505* visit in *Ghosthunting Illinois,* noting that

> *Female docents especially seem to be having a tough time with the commander's ghost. One young woman had just made a rather insulting joke about the commander... when a steel door suddenly slammed closed on her hand, injuring her. Another woman felt a hand come out of nowhere and grasp her shoulder. Of course, there was no one else in the room.*

Before the move of the *U-505* to its new site inside the Museum of Science and Industry, I spent many hours inside the sub, talking with guards and docents and taking environmental readings of the interior. Unusual effects abounded, from skewed compass readings in the 1980s and, later, spikes on my EMF meter to inexplicable pounding sounds and indistinguishable whispers near the commander's cabin.

Since the opening of the new exhibit hall and the refurbishing of the *U-505*, I've made several trips to see the sub in her new digs. Discreetly brandishing my digital thermometer, I was lucky enough to capture a fourteen degree temperature drop in the doorway of Zschech's old cabin, a change not tremendously impressive but, indeed, totally inexplicable. I was also fortunate in another respect. During one of my visits, I was the only visitor on the sub, so I was able to make a reasonable attempt to collect samples of EVP (Electronic Voice Phenomena) or possible spirit voices. Throughout the sub, I asked standard questions, such as "What is your name?" "Where are we?" "What year is it?" and "What time is it?"

Well, they say the third time's the charm, and on the third try of the latter question, outside one of the bunks, I got the most distinct EVP answer of my twenty-year career. I am familiar with simple German phrases, as my daughters attend the Saturday morning German language school at Chicago's D.A.N.K. Haus in Lincoln Square, and so, later when I played back the tape I'd made on the *U-505*, I was quick to decipher the clear words of a slow, low, male voice affirming, "einundzwanzig hundert," that is, "twenty-one hundred."

No small matter. At just after 21:00 hours on October 24, 1943, a blunt entry was made in the *U-505*'s logbook, stating only "Kommandant tot," that is, "Commanding Officer dead."

A few hours later, just before dawn according to the privately published autobiography of *U-505* crew member, Hans Goebler, "Zschech's body was lifted up to the bridge and dropped over the side without ceremony. We continued running on the surface at high speed in order to put as much distance between us and the destroyers as possible."

Though the days ahead were racked with additional depth charges and close-calls, Zschech's first officer, Paul Meyer, was able to save the *U-505*, maneuvering it out of Allied view. On the morning of November 7, the *U-505* surfaced and entered Lorient Harbor—and safety. "As we entered the harbor," writes Goebler, "...we fell out to assemble on bent knee on the upper deck... It was quite an experience... We had made it home, all of us, safe and sound. All, that is, except one." Though the men under Zschech's command admitted little sorrow at the incompetent commander's passing, the pall of his end has ever hung over the craft. Goebel writes:

> *I was never one to be frightened much by superstitions, but whenever I passed Zschech's cabin, I got goosebumps. We kept the curtain to his cabin closed, and no one had dared to enter it since the day of his suicide. Even Oberleutnant Meyer felt more comfortable staying in his junior officer's bunk. Seeing that closed curtain reminded me of the way Zschech would hide in his cabin, alone with his tortured thoughts. It was as if his ghost still haunted the little room.*

VI.

Shots in the Dark:
A Ghost Hunter's Pub Crawl

(I)t is All Souls' Night.
And two long glasses brimmed with muscatel
Bubble upon the table.
A ghost may come;
For it is a ghost's right...

—William Butler Yeats
All Souls' Night

L egendary, now, are Chicago's most established haunted pubs, taverns, and roadhouses—points of pilgrimage for natives and tourists thirsty for refreshment from both worlds.

There's the Excalibur nightclub on Dearborn, housed in the massive old Chicago Historical Society, where the misty blue figure of one of Chicago's first settlers roams the halls in search of his bones, burned when the museum's collections were destroyed in the Great Fire of 1871. A Hooter's franchise operates nearby in a structure said to be cursed. Many restaurants and bars have come and gone from the site, including Oprah Winfrey and Rich Melman's brasserie, The Eccentric, which opened in 1989—and

Photograph courtesy of David Cowan

**Excalibur nightclub in River North,
one of the city's most haunted structures.**

Photograph courtesy of Angela Larson

**Ethyl's Party,
haven for Chinatown hauntings.**

folded not long after. Interestingly, Hooter's has been going strong here for years, buoyed up in part by rumors of a phantom Hooter's Girl (I'm not making this up), who goes into the ladies' room and never comes out. There's Ole St. Andrew's Inn, still run by long-dead owner Frank Giff, who even today drains the vodka bottles at night—from behind locked cabinet doors—and feels up the female patrons, especially blondes and redheads. There's the Bucktown Pub, where former barkeep Wally committed suicide but still abuses the customers. And of course, there's Ethyl's Party (see "New Undertakings"), housed in a former Chinatown funeral home, where the dearly departed are still mixing with the regulars.

In recent years, we've lost a couple of the most atmospheric haunted pubs in Chicago: the Clark Bar, a few steps from the site of the St. Valentine's Day Massacre, frequented by the ghosts of the North Side Gang; and the infamous and much-loved Red Lion Pub, home to a host of ghosts, including the white-nightgowned wraith known as "Sharon." Despite the losses, Chicago today has no shortage of ghostly gin mills, owing to those that are regularly being added to the circuit. At these beloved spots, paranormal thrills are always on tap.

◆

The Edgewater Lounge is a favorite corner tavern in the Andersonville/Edgewater area, which once operated as a backroom speakeasy with an auto parts store fronting the place. The resident phantom is popularly believed to be that of a ghost named Mary who ran the Edgewater years ago, and who is still believed to haunt the upstairs rooms. The staff, however, begs to differ. Though they admit Mary may be a playful force here, the predominant presence is a masculine one. Dasha, a bartender at the Edgewater, talks of seeing the figure of a man at her side and sitting at the bar itself between the taps and the east end. Numerous employees and patrons have seen and sensed him, too. David, one of the bar's owners, hasn't had experiences of his own here

Photograph by the author

The Edgewater Lounge on North Ashland Avenue,
still tended by a former owner.

but is absolutely willing to believe, based on paranormal experi-

Photograph by the author

**The Fireside across the street from Rosehill Cemetery.
That's an old monument company to the left.**

ences he had in his former neighborhood home, an Edgewater coach house not far from the bar.

◆

The Fireside, on Ravenswood Avenue, sits just across the road from Rosehill Cemetery. In days gone by, mourners who made the arduous trip to the then-outlying burial ground partook of refreshment at this old roadhouse before returning home. Other travelers, it is rumored, also made visits to an upstairs brothel during their stops here. The Fireside is said to be haunted by spirits from the cemetery, as well as the phantom of a former employee or owner who fell down the steep basement stairs one night after closing. Staff members have sensed and seen the figure of a man at the foot of the stairs, where his body lay for at least a day before it was discovered.

◆

Lottie's, at Cortland and Winchester, still bears the name of the woman who made the place the center of the neighborhood's corrupted good times until the 1970s. Lottie Zagorski, a towering hermaphrodite with a bellowing voice, opened the basement of her neighborhood grocery story in the 1930s as a haven for politicians and mobsters. Whatever your vice, it was said you could find it at Lottie's, for the owner offered off-track betting, strippers, all-night poker games, booze, drugs—the works. It wasn't until 1967 that Lottie (along with mobster Andy "The Greek" Lochious) was arrested for operating a gambling ring in her basement. After her testimony before a Grand Jury in 1973, Lottie died of natural causes.

The current establishment, christened Lottie's for the beloved former matriarch, opened in the mid-1980s after several businesses came and went. In January of 2004, bones were found during a renovation of the basement. The Cook County Medical Examiner took them away. Results of the examination were inconclusive, but the renovation of Lottie's den of iniquity seemed to have stirred up her old spirit; reports of poltergeist activity and even apparitions have circulated over the past twenty years since the rehab.

◆

The Green Mill in Uptown has been a popular rest stop for weary Chicagoans since 1907, when a German beer garden operated on the premises for visitors to nearby St. Boniface Cemetery, the first German cemetery in Chicago. In 1910 the business was bought up, expanded, and renamed "The Green Mill Gardens" after the *Moulin Rouge* ("Red Gardens") in Paris. At the time, Essanay studios operated in the neighborhood, and Charlie Chaplin himself liked to take his cocktail hour at the Mill.

During Prohibition, the Green Mill was leased to the mob, and one of Capone's favorite sons, "Machine Gun Jack" McGurn, owned a share of the business. Joe E. Lewis, a regular singer at the Mill, was Capone's favorite. When he left to work a higher-paying gig downtown, it's said that McGurn ordered his tongue cut out. McGurn's men attempted the deed and beat Lewis to a pulp, but the singer survived to do stand-up comedy—at the Green Mill, of course.

Today, the Mill is still an enormously popular destination for jazz lovers, swing dancers, and anyone who can appreciate the perfectly preserved atmosphere of a posh 1930's nightclub, including the phantoms of some previous patrons. Among the paranormal activity that has been reported here is the sighting

Photograph courtesy of Angela Larson

Uptown's Green Mill,
one of Capone's favorites.

of a ghostly woman who likes to sit on the piano and footsteps still heard clattering through the underground tunnels that lead from the basement to nearby establishments, dating to the raids of Prohibition.

◆

The lobby bar in the Congress Hotel bar is one of the favorite haunts of the hotel's youngest ghost, a small boy in breeches who has been seen both on the twelfth floor (North Tower) and in many areas of the lobby. The bar is just around the corner from the elevator that takes guests to that dreadful twelfth floor where ghost hunters can find the mysteriously walled-up room believed to have inspired Stephen King's story, *1408* (see "Staying Awhile").

♦

The Liar's Club, near the intersection of Fullerton and Clybourn Avenues in Bucktown, is reputed to be haunted by a woman who was stabbed to death by her husband when the couple lived in the upstairs apartment, now part of the bar. Along with touches on the shoulder and arm, on a number of occasions patrons have reported seeing the woman's apparition leaning against the upstairs bar.

♦

The nearby California Clipper, at California Avenue and Augusta Boulevard, takes great pride in its colorful history and owns up to at least one ghost story as well. A classic "Woman in White" has been seen in a glamorous 1940s gown, in booths one and nine and on the staircase leading to the upstairs apartment. The fabulous phantom has also been known to reapply her lipstick alongside more modern party girls in the ladies' room.

♦

Chet's Melody Lounge on Archer Avenue has long been associated with the paranormal. Located across the road from the gates of Resurrection Cemetery, Resurrection Mary herself was known to have taken a cab to Chet's one blustery night years ago when a sympathetic driver picked her up along Archer in the wee hours. She told the cabbie she was going into the bar to get money to pay him. When she didn't return, the driver angrily entered the bar to demand his fare. The place was empty, save for the bartender. "No one," he said, "came in tonight." Chet's, it's been told, has long had a ghost of its own as well, and investigators have recently found some interesting evidence in the basement. A visiting clairvoyant disclosed her belief that the place is haunted by an old squatter who once lived in a shack in the adjacent woods when the area was inhabited by Native Americans. A fire destroyed his makeshift cabin one night, and it's believed that some of the wood used to build the structure which houses Chet's was wood salvaged from the fire—and haunted by the spirit of the squatter. Theory holds that the gentleman was—quite literally—very much attached to his former home and that his ghost haunts the basement here even today because of the salvaged beams.

◆

A bit farther south of Chet's on Archer Avenue stands another incredibly storied structure which occupies another sacred spot in Rez Mary history. A tavern from its inception, the building—formerly Frankie's Roadhouse, formerly Rico D's, formerly Cavallone's—sits directly across the road from the Willowbrook Ballroom, known to ghost hunters as the place where Mary danced her last dance on a fateful spring night in 1934.

The Stag's Head, an "Irish County Pub," opened at the site this summer of 2009 after Frankie's—a pizza place —was shuttered a few years ago. Former businesses have folded, one after another, on this property. Indeed, bad ventures—and vibes—seemed to curse this place time and again.

Originally operated by Capone in the 1920s, the building owns some intriguing stories. A great one tells of an afternoon in the late '20s when work was being done to expand the Willowbrook across the road. Capone himself, it is said, sent a man over to hire laborers to pour cement in the basement of the tavern.

In recent years, psychics and clairvoyants visiting the roadhouse have sensed dozens of bodies buried under the foundation, and one report tells of a previous owner who dug up the back driveway and found, underneath, cans full of hundred dollar bills. When I visited the site most recently, in the spring of 2008 to film a segment on the hauntings for a British production company, colleague Ed Shanahan and I both experienced some interesting phenomena, including the ice machine turning on while unplugged and lights and equipment malfunctioning in one of the bedrooms. In addition, Ed, a psychic feeler, felt an ominous and negative presence in the attic and on the second floor, a former brothel.

Some visitors believe that an illegitimate child, "Adam" by name, is buried in the woods behind the structure and that he may have been an unwanted offspring of Capone himself, the result of an illicit union with one of the working girls of the tavern. Adam's spirit was said to spell out messages on the floor with a set of alphabet blocks the previous staff kept in one of the bedrooms. Often, when employees would enter the room, they claimed to find that Adam had rearranged the blocks into words to express his sentiments to the living.

Adam's mother, too, is believed to haunt the structure. "Isabelle" has been seen in the women's room on the tavern level as well as on the second floor. During a previous era, a portrait hung in the dining room that was apparently found in the attic years ago. Psychics and other sensitives have matched up the painting with the ghost in question.

This whole area of Willow Springs has been known as "shady"—and haunted—for generations. Many of the businesses along the Illinois and Michigan Canal corridor feature secret basement tunnels which lead to safe houses in the area where mobsters and speakeasy clientele could retreat during Volstead-era raids. At the Stag's Head, underground tunnels lead from the bar basement to the Willowbrook Ballroom, several area farmhouses and, until recently, a family mausoleum at nearby Fairmont Hills Cemetery. The White Mausoleum, long known as a haunted site, was demolished a number of years ago, strangely close to the date businesses changed hands at the old Capone roadhouse. It was discovered that the ghostly music that had been heard drifting from the mausoleum at night was actually being carried through the underground tunnels between the roadhouse and the cemetery.

♦

For my money, the most intriguing tippling tales belong to the Tonic Room, an old tavern in Lincoln Park just down the alley next to the Biograph Theater—the same alley where John Dillinger met his end in the summer of 1934. The Tonic Room was a favorite stop for the Irish North Side Gang, which ran the illegal liquor trade here during the 1920s against Capone's South Side mob.

Even the upstairs apartments above the Tonic Room tell the story of the site's past. Every bedroom has its own entrance, evidence of their use when a brothel thrived here. When the Tonic Room was readying to open a few years ago, the staff found something bizarre in the basement. The floor, when the covering was removed, displayed a huge pentagram, and the basement ceiling had been painted with Egyptian images. After a good deal of research, a staff member discovered that the images were

Photograph by the author

**The mysterious Tonic Room
steps from the alley where Dillinger died in 1934.**

typical of those used in the rituals of the Golden Dawn, an occult group which took the fancy of Englishman Aleister Crowley. Crowley became known as the "Wickedest Man in the World" in the early-twentieth century because of his practices of bisexuality, hedonism, and other scandalous activities. Interestingly, leading members of the cult today claim that the Golden Dawn did not address the subject of sexuality in its curriculum; nonetheless, Crowley made "sex magick"—the channeling of the energy of the sex act for magical purposes—part of his own brand of the order.

Some staff members and local researchers have come to believe that the building currently housing the Tonic Room was one of the first meeting places for Crowley followers in the United States. Stories are still told, passed down through generations, of rituals that were witnessed in the basement by children, now elderly men and women, including that of a girl who claimed to have seen a woman ritually murdered in the 1930s when her father was "at a meeting" in the basement one night, presumably when the place was still—at least on the surface—a hangout for North Side gangsters. According to local tales, the occult status of the structure continued through the 1970s, when "hippies" kept up the esoteric, exploratory practices laid down by earlier cult members.

Whatever the truths behind the legends, the Tonic Room does indeed seem to host some unusual activity, including apparitions seen in the basement and in the main floor tavern and footsteps heard in the apartments upstairs.

VII.

Buying into Belief

The merchant prince, gone to dust.

—Carl Sandburg
Chicago Poems

*O*ne of the greatest misconceptions in paranormal research is that a structure must be old to be haunted. In fact, hauntings and other so-called spontaneous phenomena can occur in buildings that are quite new, including modern retail structures, like the incidents occurring at a suburban Wal-Mart, detailed in *More Chicago Haunts.*

In the far northern suburb of Crystal Lake, a Barnes & Noble bookstore has been the scene of book carts pushed by unseen hands and apports (the disappearance and reappearance of objects). Previously, the property was owned by an elderly woman who willed the property to a nearby church to be used for a school, but of course the plot was sold to developers. Employees claim to have seen the disgruntled woman's apparition in one of the bookstore's storage rooms.

Rumors abound about the CherryVale Mall in Rockford. Mall workers have experienced clothes hangers swinging on their own, items flying off racks and shelves, disembodied voices, and bathroom and changing room doors being held shut on terrified victims. Security guards have long been plagued by a nerve-wracking experience: the feeling of being followed close at their heels—sometimes all night—while making their rounds

Very recently, a friend shared the following account of an event that occurred at a JCPenney store in the Stratford Square Mall, in western suburban Bloomington:

One of my co-workers has a second job working Loss Prevention at the JCPenney store at Stratford Square. He

says there have long been nonspecific stories about eerie experiences there but nothing on which one could easily lay one's finger. People might think there is someone nearby, just looking over their shoulders, and when they turn, there is no one there. He, however, recently had an experience of a much more concrete sort. He was in the Loss Prevention Room, monitoring the cameras stationed throughout the store. One of those cameras is trained on the perfume counter because that is one of those places where small, easily-concealed objects carry a high ticket value. He literally watched as one jar of perfume sailed, all by itself, off a shelf and dove to the ground in a generous arc; it landed on the floor a couple of feet away from the shelves from which it came, not immediately before them as one would expect if it had simply toppled from its perch.

I will stress that the incident was caught on tape. He was able to go back and watch it repeatedly, and he brought in another of his LP co-workers to show him the incident. Regrettably, for proprietary reasons he could not copy the tape or bring it home. He made all reasonable efforts to come up with a prosaic reason for the incident — noting that this was a couple of days after a recent earthquake, he considered the possibility that it was the product of an aftershock, for example — but nothing proved entirely convincing. The aftershock explanation fails to explain why only this one jar of perfume fell from the shelf; moreover, this was not the most precariously positioned jar of all. Finally, if gravity alone had guided the jar to the floor, one would reasonably have expected the arc through which it fell to be far shallower, landing much nearer the base of the shelf.

◆

Of course, while stores like these have their own tales to tell, there remains a certain, more haunting aura about the great department stores of the past. No Chicago store—and few others in the world—owns as much mystique as Marshall Field & Company, now Macy's, on State Street, in the heart of the Loop.

The recent transformation of Chicago's beloved Marshall Field & Company into Macy's is now complete. The event which Field's loyal followers dreaded has come to pass, but maybe it's a good thing. Indeed, Marshall Field & Company was plagued with death and disaster—and their paranormal ramifications—for more than one hundred years.

Marshall Field was one of the city's most earnest philanthropists, and the store that he built played a major role in painting a sophisticated image of Chicago in the mind of the world, as the store's revenues provided the financial backing for some of the city's greatest and most lasting cultural institutions, including the Art Institute, the Museum of Science and Industry, the Field Museum of Natural History, and the Shedd Aquarium, named for Field's right-hand man, John G. Shedd. Field's monies also helped to sponsor the World's Columbian Exposition of 1893, which established Chicago as a major international city, and to found the University of Chicago, which remains one of the most respected institutions of higher learning in the world.

Marshall Field's success stemmed from his creativity in the world of retail, from the many innovations he introduced to the world of shopping. Field's was the first store to provide a restaurant for women shoppers in an era when it was considered uncouth for a woman to eat in public without a gentleman's company. Their pioneering tea room was established after a fed-up clerk and a weary shopper shared a chicken pot pie, still a signature dish on the Walnut Room's menu. Field's was also the first store to maintain a European buying office, the first to host bridal registries, personal shoppers, and revolving credit accounts. The store's popular book department invented the "book signing," creating excitement around new volumes by inviting authors in to meet their readers—and sell them books.

From the beginning, however, all was not beautiful. In 1902, not long after the store's opening, the *Chicago Tribune* reported that an elevator cable "gave way in an unexplained manner," causing the car to plunge ten floors, from the ninth level into the basement, killing the elevator operator and wounding one passenger.

In December 1903, the devastating fire at the nearby Iroquois Theater (now the refurbished Oriental Theater/Ford Center for the Performing Arts) took the lives of 602 Chicagoans, many of them children attending a matinée performance at the site. As the tragedy unfolded, the eighth floor of Field's was converted into a hospital where fire victims were bandaged with dishtowels from

Photograph courtesy of Michael Spudic

The Oriental Theater (formerly the Iroquois Theater site). Victims of the 1903 theater fire were taken to Marshall Field & Co. on the corner.

the housewares department. Those who died during treatment were wrapped in sheets and blankets from the bedding department to await the coroner's wagons. The *Chicago Tribune* reported, the day after the disaster, that

> *(t)he west room and employees' sitting room on the eighth floor were filled within thirty minutes after the work of rescue began. Anxious men seeking relatives and friends pushed their way through the crowd. One had heard that his wife and boy had been taken to the store. He found his son safe, but the search for the woman failed.*

> *...One woman, whose two children had not been heard from, went into convulsions, and another half dragged*

Photograph courtesy of Michael Spudic

Macy's (Marshall Field & Co.)
In 1903, the 8th floor was used as a temporary morgue.

*and half carried in her two children, whose clothing had
been almost all torn off of them.*

Despite the dramatic events of the store's early years, no
tragedy could personally compare to that which befell the family
in 1905. That year, Marshall Field Jr. was found shot to death
in the bedroom of his own home on Chicago's Prairie Avenue,
reportedly the result of a self-inflicted shotgun wound. Field's
family told police the death had been an accident; Marshall had
been cleaning a hunting weapon when it accidentally discharged.
Neighbors weren't so sure, however, and the press soon leaked
rumors of Field's longtime dealings in the old Levee vice district,
where Chinatown sprawls today. Had Field taken his own life to
bow out of some untoward matter at Chicago's most prestigious
brothel, the Everleigh Club? No one really knows, but we do
know that for a century the enormous Field Jr. house (known as
the Murray house from its first owner) stood abandoned; no one,
it seems, could live in it.

That is, until now.

For the past several years, the thirty thousand square foot
property at 1919 South Prairie has undergone massive gutting
and reconstruction. The original forty-three rooms, fourteen
fireplaces, and nine baths have been transformed into six condo-
miniums, with price tags of 870 thousand to 1.7 million dollars.
But are the new tenants really comfortable?

Not necessarily.

Along with the sinister mark of its previous tenant, the house
bears another burden. Like the rest of Prairie Avenue, it was
originally built on the killing fields of the Fort Dearborn Massacre of 1812. That Anglo-Indian battle resulted in the scalping and
killing of scores of Chicago settlers whose bodies remained on
the windswept sand dunes for four years until soldiers returned
to the burned-out fort to rebuild it in 1816.

At the turn of the nineteenth century, Prairie Avenue dwell-
ers were already complaining about the paranormality of their

Photograph by the author

The Marshall Field Jr. Mansion before its renovation.

lovely digs. Today, with a new generation of affluence moving in, the new life in the neighborhood is joined, again, by the dead. Owners of the fabulous town homes and modern mansions on Prairie have already whispered about unseen presences in their opulent homes: footsteps that come and go without a trace, sounds of weeping and singing when no one is near, even full-fledged apparitions of "settlers" or "pioneers."

The home of the Field family business, too, continues today a legacy of death that began more than a century ago. Throughout the years, from the 1920s and well into the '60s, rumors arose of a number of employee suicides said to have occurred from the eighth level of the open-air atrium in Marshall Field & Company; coworkers were said to claim that the victims had all spoken of a "heaviness" or depression while working on that floor. Could the use of the floor as a hospital—and morgue—for the Iroquois fire victims have left some kind of deadly impression on the building itself? No one can know for sure, but there seemed to be no stopping the macabre events.

In 1972, a car rammed a crowd of pedestrians on the south side of the Marshall Field and Company store, continuing through a display window, killing one shopper and injuring seven others.

In 1973, almost exactly a year later, a North Side Chicago woman jumped to her death from the ninth floor of the landmark building, leaving behind a suicide note in the housewares department.

The sale, then, of the State Street store in 2004 to Macy's made some paranormal experts wonder: would the change bring an end to the Field family curse as well?

Photograph courtesy of Michael Spudic

Interior of Macy's, formerly Marshall Field & Co.

Apparently not.

In the summer of 2007, a man entered Macy's just before closing time and—according to employees—purchased a white suit, white hat, white shoes and gloves. He donned his purchases in the men's room, rode the elevator to the eighth floor, and leaped to his death from the atrium rail, ending up splayed across the Coach handbag display.

The tragedy surrounding the Marshall Field family and its world-famous department store has led some paranormal investigators to speculate on the reasons for the problem. Many Chicagoans believe that the trouble may stem from Field Sr.'s life of luxury on the Fort Dearborn Massacre site, sacred ground for Native Americans. Could Field have built his mansion, as some claim, on the mass grave of the Native American dead?

Today, the proud and historic shell of the world's first modern department store has a new resident from New York, and though the store pays a lot of lip service to the "legacy" of the great Marshall Field & Company, the new bosses likely have little idea of the history—and mystery—they've inherited.

VIII.

New Undertakings

Take a hold now
On the silver handles here,
Six silver handles,
One for each of his old pals.
Take him on the last haul,
To the cold straight house,
The level even house,
To the last house of all.

—Carl Sandburg
Chicago Poems

$\mathcal{F}$uneral homes are an obvious choice for ghost hunting, though not necessarily for seasoned ghost hunters. Regular researchers believe that ghosts are more likely to remain attached to the places they frequented in life or to the site where they met their end, violent or otherwise. Sometimes funeral homes do, indeed, seem to hold on to the souls whose bodies they have ushered out of the sight of the living, even after they have passed out of service to the dead.

The 2009 film *A Haunting in Connecticut* retold, in Hollywood fashion, reportedly true events that occurred in an old funeral home in Southington, Connecticut, as told by the Snedecker family, who moved into the now-defunct mortuary to live in 1986. The case was famously investigated by Lorraine Warren and her

Photograph courtesy of Angela Larson

Ethyl's Party
A ghost joins the jam sessioins.

135

late husband, Ed, who claimed that the house was inhabited by a number of restless spirits and at least one demon. Though much controversy and accusations of fraud surrounded the case, the Snedeckers held to their horrific stories of the place, including reports of apparitions, poltergeist activity, and even supernatural rape and sodomy. According to local rumors, one of the erstwhile morticians had been accused of necrophilia, and the Snedeckers claimed that soon after their move into the house one of their sons had started writing poetry with necrophilic themes.

The most famous of Chicago's haunted erstwhile funeral homes is the old Colletta's Funeral Home in Chinatown, now operating as a tavern called Ethyl's Party. Apparitions have been seen of a trench-coated figure at the bar, and occasionally an "extra member" will be seen playing with the bands that perform in the alcove where bodies were once displayed. The television and jukebox, too, seem to have minds of their own, turning on and off randomly without the help of earthly hands.

◆

Photograph courtesy of Angela Larson

Mrs. Murphy's Bistro
A beautiful eatery with a disturbing history.

Surprisingly, a number of successful restaurants have made their homes in former funeral homes, including Mrs. Murphy & Sons Irish Bistro on Lincoln Avenue. When I was a girl, my police officer father used to tell stories about this place. Specifically, he would remind my mother that when he died, he should not be sent there, as police had been called at some point to investigate claims of necrophilia by one of the employees who had been hired by the family. Sporadic reports of mild paranormal activity have helped to make the lavishly remodeled interior even more atmospheric.

◆

Ann Sather's, a true institution on Belmont Avenue in Lakeview, now has a number of other locations, including smaller cafés that dot Chicago's trendy neighborhoods. The original restaurant was run by Swedish immigrants from a small storefront near the Belmont elevated train stop, and Ann Sather purchased it in the 1940s and made it a neighborhood favorite. After several years of operating in the cramped quarters, new owner Tom Tunney (now the ward's alderman) moved the restaurant into the old Hursen Funeral Home, several doors west. The macabre past of the site

Photograph courtesy of Angela Larson

Comedy Sportz, formerly Ann Sather's, on Belmont Avenue.

did not deter hungry diners, despite rumors that the old embalming room had become the bustling new kitchen.

Bodies were actually embalmed upstairs before being brought back down to the viewing parlor. Tunney says that the number one thing people asked about was whether his restaurant used the same coolers Hursen's had, though no such coolers existed; bodies were immediately embalmed. Rumors circulated through the North Side that poltergeist activity and even an apparition or

Photograph courtesy of Angela Larson

Old Town Tatu, formerly Klemundt Funeral Home.

two were not uncommon while Ann Sather's operated in the old parlor, but Tunney family members and other employees deny having experienced anything unusual.

◆

Old Town Tatu's building dates to the late 1800s when the Klemundt Funeral Parlor operated out of the Victorian structure. Rumor has it that a cemetery also operated behind the property, though research on this is inconclusive. What's not inconclusive is ghost hunting efforts. It's even said that the shop's founder, the late Rich "Tapeworm" Herrera, may have made good on his promise to come back after death to scare the other ghosts away. Keys skid off the counter, and a mask on the wall has flown off repeatedly. Employees also talk about activity in the upstairs apartment, including one incident where the dog was found locked out on the back porch by unseen hands after a witness heard the sound of the door opening and closing. Investigators have also reportedly made contact with a man named "Walter" in the basement via voice recording (EVP). Walter was the name of the original parlor owner.

♦

The Twelve-Step House on Damen Avenue is a meeting center for Alcoholics Anonymous and also a halfway house where those in recovery can live for a short period of time. Some residents have wondered if they have extra support from the dead who were embalmed here before 1976, when the former funeral home closed. The basement meeting room which once housed the embalming area is one which members describe as terminally

Photograph by the author

Recovering wraiths?
The 12-Step House on North Damen Avenue.

cold and with a "heavy presence," and the basement toilet has been heard flushing by itself. A former custodian often saw a figure walking through the area after the house had been locked at night. On the second floor, where the dormitory area is located, appliances have been known to turn on and off by themselves.

◆

Without question, the most beautiful former funeral home in Chicago was not originally a funeral home at all, but the Krause Music Store at 4611 North Lincoln Avenue. Designed by masterful architect Louis Sullivan, the store's owner killed himself in an upstairs apartment just a handful of years after the business opened. Thereafter, an undertaker set up shop in the structure, installing a casket elevator to move basement embalming to the second-floor chapel. After the parlor closed, a number of business

Photograph by the author

Krause Music Store in Lincoln Square.

moved in and out until the building was purchased by its current owners, Peter and Pooja Vukosavich. Today, the totally rehabbed structure houses their design firm, Studio V, on the first floor and a refurbished apartment upstairs. When the couple first bought the property, before its restoration, there was a first order of business: drive away the evil spirits.

The *Chicago Tribune* talked to the couple in 2007 for a July 29 piece on the restoration. Their reporter, Blair Kamin, found that, from the start, Pooja felt a sadness in the building, and Peter agreed to perform a number of rituals to drive away evil spirits that Pooja felt had taken over. They circled each room with salt and rice according to the advice of a feng shui master, burned herbs according to Hindu tradition, and meditated to encourage the stability and peace of the place. The casket elevator was also removed, and today, the Krause building is believed to be inhabited by only the living.

IX.

Final Judgments

I will show you fear in a handful of dust.

—T.S. Eliot
The Waste Land: I. The Burial Of The Dead

*O*ne of Chicago's most recognized locations is the intersection of Twenty-sixth Street and California Avenue—a.k.a. "26th and Cal" or simply "26th Street"—home of the Cook County Criminal Courthouse and its adjoining jail. A major player in Chicago's dramatic history, the jail has held some of the nation's most notorious inmates, from gangland kingpins Al Capone, Tony Accardo, and Frank Nitti, to modern-day monsters like Richard Speck and John Wayne Gacy.

Cook County, the Illinois county which includes Chicago and many of its surrounding suburbs, was founded in the early 1830s with unincorporated Chicago as its county seat. Chicago's

Photograph courtesy of Angela Larson

The Cook County Criminal Courthouse.
If walls could talk...

first jailhouse was not erected until 1835, some two years after the city's incorporation, but by mid-century the tiny stockade that Chad served until then could no longer accommodate the escalating crime rates of the burgeoning county seat.

A larger jail was then created which sat near the Chicago River at present-day Hubbard Street, and inmates from the old prison were brought over to the new in the midst of the dedication ceremonies. The *Chicago Tribune* wrote of one Joseph Gilholley's move to the new jail

> *...during the noon recess. As the guard escorted him across the court, he heard the sounds of the banqueters who were dedicating the new building, and he tried to wrest himself away from the bailiff. Finally he was placed again in his cell and the guard went to get him his luncheon and returned with a tin vessel containing hot soup. When it was handed to him he hurled the contents of the bowl in the guard's face and then belabored him over the head with the empty dish. He was placed in the dungeon.*

Despite the "bright cells and fresh, clean beds" and "an up-to-date fumigation" (*Chicago Tribune* 7/11/1897) for each new prisoner's clothes, the new jail had room for only the city's most dangerous criminals, whose trials were staged at the courthouse next door. Much like today, the guilty were sent away to live out their sentences at state penitentiaries. Those who had been arrested for less serious crimes were thrown in Chicago's bridewell, the city's common lockup in the heart of the vice district, near Polk and Wells Streets.

By 1871, the bridewell had been given new digs at Twenty-sixth Street and California Avenue—and a new name: The Chicago House of Corrections. In that devastating year of the Great Fire, inmate populations swelled at both the new House of Corrections and the Hubbard Street jail. When the riverside jail could no longer accommodate the rising crowds, a new county jail was built next to the city lockup at 26th and Cal. By 1930, the two jails were in full operation, and the Cook County Criminal Courthouse had been erected next door, making for a simple transition from arrest to hearing and trial.

By the 1950s, overcrowding was threatening the smooth operation of the Chicago-based criminal court system, as the jails were now holding sentenced criminals as well as those awaiting hearings and trials. Adding to the numbers were those on death row—inmates who had previously been sent away for execution by the state but who were now executed on site at Twenty-sixth Street

Finally, after two decades of chaos, at the dawn of the 1970s, the Illinois State Legislature created the Cook County Department of Corrections, effectively merging the two separate jails into one institution. To aid with overcrowding, federal monies were secured to create the modern jail buildings that stand today, accommodating almost ten thousand inmates daily.

I talked at length with Mike, a lifelong resident of West Rogers Park, who has served as a deputy sheriff at the Criminal Courts for a number of years, following in the footsteps of his father, who worked here for decades and loved the job. With the passage of time, both generations of deputies became well acquainted with the ebb and flow of human life at the IDOC—and with some troubled souls who have come and *not* gone.

One night, while working Midnights in March of 2006, Mike was sitting just inside the front doors of the courthouse with absolutely no one else around when an experience began that he'll never forget:

> *Twenty feet to the right were file cabinets where people kept their stuff they didn't want to take home with them. There were styrofoam cups on the file cabinet. All the doors were closed—no air, no nobody. Three A.M. I start hearing a goofy melody of whistling. Figured someone was screwing with me. Called the office: "Why are you screwing with me?" The whistling starts again. I thought*

the floor guy was mopping the floor. Nobody. Gone for the night. The hallway leads from the public bathrooms to the stairwell. I got up and checked it out—the bathrooms, the stairs. Nobody. Sat back down. A second later, the whistling got louder, and—all of the sudden—the styrofoam cups went flying.

Mike reminded me about the unique nature of the courthouse's past, as the jail—and its world-famous gallows—all once occupied the same property. Today, criminals awaiting trial at the Cook County Criminal Courts Building are held at the relatively new jail next door, but those who are sentenced are sent to serve at outlying Illinois penitentiaries.

There are so many times walking through that building at night where you just feel it. There has been so much weird stuff that's happened there. It's not like most places where you go from jail to prison; it was all in the same place. If you were sentenced, you were going right to death.

You'd expect a trove of ghost stories here, and the place doesn't disappoint. Yet, many of the haunting experiences here—of attorneys, judges and staff—are like dreams, without any known history behind them. Mike talks of a

buddy (who) used to sit on the third floor of the administration building. One night he starts hearing moaning. This guy's by no means strange about anything—doesn't believe in this stuff or talk about it. Things are what they are. There was no wind—would not have been pressure on the windows. He wondered if someone got accidentally locked in here. (He) walked the whole jury room until six A.M. and never saw anyone. He said it was the scariest thing on earth.

◆

Photograph by the author

The Pinecrest Apartments at the lakefront, home to William Heirens' second victim, Frances Brown. Police found the words, "For heaven's sake catch me before I kill more." written in lipstick on the living room wall.

The courthouse is filled with dreadful memories—the stuff, literally, of Chicago's nightmares. There is the room where, on September 4, 1946, William Heirens—the "Lipstick Killer"— pled guilty to three murders, including the dismemberment of six-year-old Suzanne Degnan, attempted to hang himself in the adjoining jail the same night. There is the courtroom where, in 1966, Richard Speck calmly sat through testimony condemning him and his eight abominable slayings. There is the hall of sorrow where John Wayne Gacy was tried, the trial spanning those heartbreaking five weeks in 1980. Even now, thirty years later, Mike reports, "They claim the room is haunted by the kids. They hear giggling, running around, shuffling around the benches, as if (they) were fidgeting in court."

Gacy, like most maximum security risks, would have been held in the spare, foreboding chamber known as "The Max," a steel-walled cell with gates at either end. Today, after years of harboring the penned-in anxiety of killers—and worse—the Max has its own memories. Stories abound of disembodied voices, singing, or crying. Dark figures glide effortlessly through its walls. Lights fail.

Legends run rampant through the unfathomable history—and elusive physical makeup—of the Criminal Courts. As Mike says, "Twenty-sixth Street is weird. They don't take anything out. They just put stuff in." Anything no longer in service, they say, is simply locked up or closed off, but remains.

The most notorious of these spaces was Division One. Mike has never seen it himself, but

> *(the) electricians talk about it. When they talk about seclusion it was literally dog cages in Division One. I've heard this through stories only. They called it "The Hole." You literally couldn't move.*

Particularly puzzling is the courthouse's eighth floor, completely closed off for years from public and staff access. According to oral accounts that still pass among the staff, the eighth floor served as a morgue until fifty years ago. Backing up the rumors are reports of paranormal activity: sounds of commotion from behind the locked doors.

One of the courthouse's many secrets was brought to light in 2006 when the jail's storied gallows were put up for auction with a starting bid of five thousand dollars. The world-famous Cook County gallows were originally built to execute the anarchists associated with the 1886 Haymarket Riot. Between those first executions and the last, in 1927, the gallows ushered in the deaths of more than eighty men.

After the last hanging, the county disallowed death by hanging in favor of the electric chair; however, a curious circumstance kept the structure on site—in the jailhouse basement, to be exact—for fifty more years. In 1921, "Terrible" Tommy O'Connor escaped from the Cook County Jail just days before his anticipated execution. (The story of Tommy O'Connor was first made famous by Chicago journalist Ben Hecht in *The Front Page* which was adapted for the screen in *His Girl Friday*.) As his sentence specified death by hanging, the county kept the gallows at Twenty-sixth Street just in case O'Connor was ever caught. Finally, in 1977, a judge deemed that the capture of O'Connor would likely never be realized. He ordered the gallows to be sold.

The gallows went—then, without a ripple—to Mike Donley, who operates Wild West Town in the village of Union, Illinois, about an hour northwest of Chicago. When, in 2006, Donley pronounced the attraction too macabre for the youthful patrons of his Union museum, he put the gallows back on the auction block.

Unlike the first sale, the gallows had many offers the second time around, including that of Libby Mahoney, chief curator of the Chicago History Museum, who wanted to make the structure part of a permanent Haymarket Riot exhibit, and longtime American exploiter of the strange, Ripley's Believe It or Not. In the end, the gallows sold to Ripley's for nearly $70,000, disappointing the many historical associations, labor unions, and opponents of capital punishment who'd hoped for a more educational installation of the gruesome artifact.

Mark of the Devil

Sometimes evil makes itself known. Pictures of the devil make it easy to identify what evil looks like. In our everyday world, sometimes evil is harder to find, moving among us. Then sometimes evil comes out of the shadows, and the results are literally deadly.

Such was the case with one of Chicago's most notorious mass murderers, Richard Speck. A drifter and ne'er-do-well with a pock-marked face and a sinister desire to become famous, Speck became famous for the murder of eight nursing students on

Chicago's South Side in 1966. Born December 6, 1941, in Kirkwood, Illinois, Richard Speck lived a rather nondescript early life, sharing a home with six older siblings and one younger sister. By all accounts, Speck was close to his father, with whom he often went fishing. Many have blamed the events of his later life on the untimely death of his beloved father when Richard was seven years old and on the austere upbringing he received from his mother until her remarriage to a alcoholic who terrorized Richard during his drinking bouts. Whatever the reasons, Speck's later life was to be marred by his inability to "fit in" into society. Rather, he constantly lurked ominously outside it. He seemed to be waiting for his moment.

Speck's mother, a religious zealot, married Carl Lindberg shortly after her husband's death, moving the family to Dallas, Texas. Here Speck again failed to make any effort at school or friendships and had no real interests. It was not long before, as a teenager, he dropped out of high school and followed a group of petty criminals in a life of small-time crime. He broke into houses and committed robberies after mastering the art of the switchblade. While in Dallas, in 1961, he met and married Shirley Malone. She was already pregnant with his daughter, a child Speck would never meet. Malone divorced Speck in 1966 after he had spent most of their married life in jail.

During this early criminal period, Speck had his first experience as a violent offender. Late one night, after hours of drinking, he accosted a woman in a Dallas parking lot and tried to rape her at knifepoint. The woman got away and was able to testify on the attack. Speck was arrested.

In 1965, Speck reappeared in his hometown. Some believe he returned in an attempt to relive his happy days of youth, before his father had died He began drinking heavily in bars and began using narcotics. One night, in a local tavern, Speck bragged to bar patrons that he nearly killed a woman in Dallas. Accordingly, he began to earn a local reputation for trouble. When a sixty-five-year-old woman named Mrs. Virgil Harris was raped and robbed, it was not long before the police were looking for Speck. While she was attacked from behind, the one clear description she could give of her attacker was his slow, southern drawl. Speck went on the run, later turning to his family for help.

Richard had a sister, Martha, who lived in Chicago with her husband, Gene Johnson, and the two took in the refugee. Gene did his best to get Speck a job, but after several brushes with trouble, he was fired from all of them. In fact, during this time his stint as a merchant seaman was the longest and last employment he would have. He was fired from his job on a Lake Michigan ship after he pulled a knife on a superior. Gene tried to get Speck another job, but while awaiting word on it, Speck was lured by the promise of violence once again.

During his bouts of unemployment, Speck spent much time at down at the Maritime Union Hall in the Jeffrey Manor neighborhood. Across the street from the hall was a townhouse at 2319 East One Hundredth Street. Speck had spent the morning of July 13, 1966 outside this apartment building watching the student nurses from South Chicago Community Hospital who lived there come and go between classes. Late in the morning, Speck received word that the job he was waiting for was given to another seaman with more seniority.

That afternoon, after a desperate phone call to Martha, Speck met his sister at the Maritime Union Hall, and she gave him twenty-five dollars. He then went from bar to bar, following a woman who would become another of his rape victims. By eleven o'clock that evening, Speck was on his way to his most violent, most heinous, most notorious crime—one that would haunt Chicago history forever.

Just after the hour, Richard made his way from the nearby Shipyard Inn, where he was boarding, to the townhouse at 2319 East One Hundredth Street. He broke the kitchen window with the handle of his switchblade and entered the darkened home. The first person he came across was Corazon Amurao, a Filipino exchange student. Speck forced her into one of the bedrooms upstairs with a gun he had stolen from the woman he'd raped earlier that day. He gathered the other women in the townhouse and forced them into the largest of the bedrooms. Upon entering, Richard had initially encountered six nursing students. At around 11:40, a seventh girl, Gloria Davy, came in from a date with her fiancé. Speck corralled her in the bedroom with the others.

He began by telling the women he was after money, that he was down on his luck and needed some cash. At gunpoint, the young women were quick to give him what they had. Speck made small talk with them, chatting as though he had nothing sinister on his mind. Then, suddenly, he rose and began cutting the bed-sheets into strips, which he used to bind the girls.

Beginning with Pamela Wilkening, who spit in Speck's face and told him she would pick him out of a lineup, Speck took the nurses one by one into neighboring rooms where he performed atrocities on them. While he was attempting to rape Wilkening, however, he was surprised by two other nurses who came into the apartment, unaware of the horror that was already going on. Before they could flee, Speck stabbed each of them nearly twenty times.

Over the course of the next four hours, Speck raped, beat, strangled, stabbed, or cut the throats of the innocent nurses until eight of them were dead. He even took the time to wipe the blood from his hands and knife between each murder. While Speck went from room to room, the women attempted to crawl under the beds to hide. He repeatedly pulled them out from under, thinking he had gotten them all.

In the early morning hours of July 14, Speck left the house through the front door and lit a cigarette. After strolling to the Calumet River to dispose of the bloody knife, Speck went back to his room at the Shipyard Inn and went to sleep, thinking he had committed the perfect crime.

While the city was waking, from under the bed in the largest townhouse bedroom crawled Corazon Amurao. The slight woman had survived the horrors of the night, and now she climbed out

Photograph courtesy of Angela Larson

**The Jeffrey Manor townhouse (first on the left)
where the Speck Murders occurred.**

onto the window ledge, her screams of "Help me! Help me! They're all dead!" echoing through the neighborhood.

In the townhouse next door, among the rooms at another student dorm for the South Chicago Community Hospital, a young nurse named Judy Dykton heard the screaming Amurao above the hum of a fan and went outside. She entered the neighboring house and found, in the living room, Gloria Davy, the first of Speck's victims, lying facedown on the sofa. She had been raped, sodomized, and strangled. During Dykton's discovery of the crimes, Speck was one mile from the scene, in a bar, drinking.

Outside, a police cruiser had turned the corner and come up the street. Seeing Amurao on the ledge, Officer Daniel Kelly pulled over and approached the house, radioing for help. Kelly recognized Davy and radioed dispatch, screaming, "I know her!" The officer had once dated Davy's sister.

Speck thought he had killed all the nurses who could have served as witnesses against him. He believed he would get away with what was being called "The Crime of the Century." What Speck did not realize was that there was an eyewitness to the crime. Corazon Amurao had crawled under the bed while Speck came and went from the other rooms. He had apparently lost count of the number of women he held captive and did not notice she was missing. Amurao was able to provide police with not only a description of what Speck looked like but with the most telling piece of evidence for Speck's identification: a now-legendary tattoo that read "Born to Raise Hell."

When Speck found out about Amurao, he panicked. The police were able to lift fingerprints from the scene—from a bloody handprint on the door of the bedroom—and with the eyewitness description, newspapers and television reports were quickly circulating pictures of Speck and word of the distinctive tattoo.

Speck made his way north to Skid Row and rented a room for ninety cents a day. Using the name R. Franklin, he tried to keep a low profile as Chicago police were stopping anyone trying to use the subway, buses, or trains, in the hopes of spotting this most notorious suspect. Speck, however, was not planning on going to jail.

The following day, Speck drank a gallon of wine and smashed the bottle in his seedy room. Every violent act Speck committed required his total inebriation, and his next was no exception. He used the broken glass to slash his wrist and arm then waited to bleed to death. His plan would have worked had it not been for a handyman who called the police to try to save Speck's life. Neither the handyman nor the police recognized Speck, and he was taken to Cook County Hospital.

While cleaning Speck's wounds, under blood caked and dried on Speck's forearm, the attending doctor uncovered the telltale tattoo. He recognized it at once and informed the police that this was the man they were looking for. Without a word, Speck was sent to a hospital bed for recovery. Not long after, dressed in her nursing uniform, Corazon Amurao walked determinedly into Speck's room and pointed him out to police as the man who had killed her friends.

Speck never confessed to the crime to his lawyer, the police, or the media. With fingerprints lifted from the crime scene and with the help of prints on file with the Dallas police department, Speck was tied to the crime with hard evidence. Together with the eyewitness account, the state had an open and shut case against Speck for the murder of eight young women.

Speck's trial had to be moved to Peoria, Illinois, more than two hours south of Chicago, far from the media and notoriety of the Chicago scene where the murders took place. While in jail, however, questions arose as to Speck's ability to stand trial. Was he insane to commit a crime like this? He claimed repeatedly that he was unable to remember what happened that night. He blamed his inability to remember on the fact that he was drunk and suffered alcoholic blackouts. The court ruled that he was able to stand trial for the crimes, and in December of 1966 the trial of Richard Franklin Speck began.

Speck showed not a shred of remorse. In fact, while in court he appeared disinterested in the grisly proceedings. At a key moment, Corazon Amurao was brought into the courtroom and, after substantial testimony, was asked to identify the man who murdered her roommates. Without hesitation, she got up from the witness stand, walked across the room, stood right in front of Speck and pointed her finger in his face. "That is the man," she stated.

Based on the physical evidence and Amurao's valiant testimony, the jury took forty-nine minutes to convict Speck on April 15, 1967, and to recommend the death penalty.

After several appeals the capital sentence was overturned. Speck's lawyers claimed that certain potential jurors were excluded from the process and that their inclusion would have changed Speck's sentence. The sentence was changed to 400 to 1200 years in prison, a minimum of fifty years for each murder. Speck would spend the rest of his life behind bars in one of the toughest prisons in the United States, the Stateville Penitentiary in Joliet, Illinois.

Speck worked hard to survive in prison, as those who committed violent crimes against women were usually treated very brutally on death row. He sought the protection of prison guards and eventually began injecting female hormones which caused him to grow breasts so he would be attractive to other inmates. A shocking jailhouse video surfaced five years after Speck's death which shows him hideously transformed, wearing women's underwear, snorting cocaine with another inmate, yet unrepentant.

On December 5, 1991, Richard Speck died of a heart attack one day before his fiftieth birthday. No one claimed his body. He was cremated and his ashes scattered over an undisclosed location near Joliet, Illinois. Speck's sister, when notified by the coroner, said she would not claim him. She tells her children never to tell anyone that their uncle was Richard Speck.

Several attempts have been made to try to find reasons for Speck's gruesome crimes. In the 1960s a theory surfaced that he was what some call a "supermale." Men with this classification, it was suggested, possess the XYY chromosome rather than the usual XY. The study of the supermale, which included men on death row and those convicted of other violent crimes, showed that they all possessed this same genetic anomaly. The theory was later discredited as bunk science.

During an autopsy, portions of Speck's brain were removed and studied. After studying what they believed to be abnormally developed and underdeveloped portions of his brain, medical examiners from all over the country agreed that the neural abnormalities Richard Speck exhibited were among the most severe they had ever seen.

Strange stories circulated after Speck's arrest. According to legend, witnesses claimed to still see him in the places he liked to frequent—including the flophouses and taverns where he spent his last days at large. Some even claimed to have spoken to him on the street—while he was being held in the Cook County Jail. Reports of such "phantasms of the living" occur most commonly during times of acute stress or crisis, or in cases where there is mental illness in the person sighted. Some researchers theorize that anomalies in the brain of the mentally ill person may somehow allow the individual to project themselves to remote places, either physically or, more probably, by creating a psychic impression that can be picked up by psychically sensitive viewers.

Rumors still circulate about the cell where Speck was held at the Cook County Jail. Some say that a number of prisoners held in the cell committed suicide after feeling acutely agitated or angry, causing administrators to stop housing inmates in it "as a precaution." According to urban legend, it remains unused even today, despite severe overcrowding.

Miles away, the townhouse at 2319 East One Hundredth Street still stands, amazingly, inhabited. The tenants don't talk about the events of 1966; rather, they are openly hostile to curiosity-seekers hopeful to win their way in for a tour or even a word.

I've driven down to the far Southeast Side many times to retrace the steps of Richard Speck and to wonder about what went on in his thoughts that day and after. I think about Corzaon Amurao, valiantly slipping under the lower bunk amid the horror of that night and surviving to tell the tale. I've taken many photographs of the building: the kitchen window where Speck entered, the front door by which Judy Dykton first came upon the unfathomable scene, the ledge outside the upper windows, where Amurao stood and screamed as the sun rose. To me, you'd never know by looking at the place that anything untoward had happened there.

Many times, though, over the years, I've shown my photographs to those interested in such things.

Some see, in the windows, the face of the Devil himself.

The Barber of Riverside

The "Chicago Outfit" was for generations the most powerful organized crime syndicate in the country, Al Capone the most infamous gang boss that ever lived. Capone's name and legacy are known all over the world, but what of those who came after him? The press put a former barber, Frank Nitti, in charge of the Chicago Outfit, but things weren't exactly what they seemed.

Capone had successfully taken over the prime liquor distribution racket during prohibition, cornered the market on prostitution in the old Levee district and other dens around the city, and organized the independent small operations competing with him. The downfall of Capone came, not from police or a rival's bullet, but from the IRS, when he was imprisoned after the St. Valentine's Day Massacre—for tax evasion. After the arrest, everyone wondered who would lead.

Frank Nitti, born Francesco Rafaele Nitto in 1886, practiced as a humble barber at the start of his career. An immigrant from Sicily, Nitti appeared in Chicago after serving the Five Points Gang in New York, Capone's alma mater from his pre-Chicago days. Nitti was a well-known fence for stolen goods, and he seemed to have a nose for finding markets for bootleg whiskey. He caught the attention of Capone and John Torrio, Capone's predecessor. Adding to his savvy was a genuine trustworthiness and likeability. Capone liked Nitti, and Nitti liked the connections and esteem of the affiliation.

As Nitti rose through the ranks of Capone's operation, he gained the nickname "The Enforcer." He never really got his hands dirty, but he made sure those who owed paid. By the time he died, Nitti had an estimated twenty-five corpses on his resume. While the part he played in the St. Valentine's Day Massacre is still unclear, he has been given credit in a number of films and television shows as a mastermind behind, if not triggerman at, the deadly event. Despite his shadowy role in the massacre, one job was his alone, and undisputedly: the murder of rival gangster, Hymie Weiss.

On North State Street, between Chicago Avenue and Superior Street, towers Holy Name Cathedral. Across the street from this illustrious landmark was Schofield's Flower Shop, a legitimate business but also the headquarters of the North Side

(Irish) mob leader, Dion O'Bannion. So-called "Florist to the Mob," O'Bannion used to boast that he could give a mobster the most elaborate funeral money could buy, and for just a little extra he'd even provide the body. When O'Bannion was killed in the shop by South Side rivals in 1924, the operation fell to Weiss, and he still maintained the Schofield's front.

Next door to the flower shop was a rather nondescript building that advertised rooms for rent. On October 5, 1926, a fair haired, light skinned gentleman rented one of the rooms facing the back alley with the stipulation that should a street-side room with a view become available, he'd like that one instead. Days later, after procuring the room, he left the establishment—and the room in the care of "two dark skinned, dark haired gentlemen." These men occupied the room until the morning of October 11, watching the happenings on State Street, particularly at Schofield's flower shop.

On the morning of October 11, Weiss and several companions parked their car on Superior Street just in the shadows of Holy Name Cathedral. Before they had a chance to cross the street, shots rang out from the rooming house window across the street. One of the two men employed a shotgun, the other a Thompson sub-machine gun with a hundred-round drum. They hit Weiss's companion seven times, and he staggered to the ground, dying almost instantly. Within minutes, Weiss lay motionless on the pavement; the twenty-eight-year-old boss was dead. The remaining four members of his entourage ducked behind the corner of the cathedral from which they had come, onto Superior Street. Interestingly, slugs became lodged in the cornerstone of the cathedral, and the telltale bullet holes remain even today, despite reported attempts of the Archdiocese to plug them. It's rumored that no mortar will harden, and that perhaps some paranormal presence is still stirring here.

The killing of Weiss was a coup for Capone. Weiss was one of the few Capone truly feared. In a time when gangsters were gunned down by nameless assassins seemingly weekly, Nitti became notorious for the "second floor front type ambush." This technique would later be employed, though with variations, at the famous St. Valentine's Day Massacre. Nitti had orchestrated what became known in gangland lore as "the perfect execution."

After Capone's imprisonment, Nitti took over Chicago, but it was no longer the city Capone had conquered. The end of Prohibition also meant the end of whiskey trafficking—and the easy money they supplied. Big business was the wave of the Outfit's future, and Nitti was in for the long haul, or so he thought. When the feds caught wind of an Outfit plan to extort Hollywood millions, Nitti knew his time was up and that he'd soon be back in Leavenworth prison or, worse, with Capone on "the Rock" at Alcatraz Island.

On the evening of March 19, 1943, Frank left his home in the lovely suburb of Riverside, just west of Chicago, to go for an evening walk. He made his way to the Illinois Central Railroad tracks near Harlem and Twenty-second Street (Cermak Road). A gunshot brought the attention of railway workers, but before they could reach him, Nitti had shot himself—fatally—in the temple. Ever since, walkers and drivers along Cermak have seen a figure walking westward, head down, near the site where Nitti took his life.

Meat is Murder

Just southwest of Chicago proper lies a sprawling expanse of slough-studded forest, one of the largest preserve areas in northern Illinois and, many believe, one of the most haunted regions in America.

Though the story to be told plays out in one of this area's many villages, it cannot be told without setting the larger scene because Palos Park is nestled in one of the nation's most mysterious districts, and Chicago's most supernatural realm.

The area known locally as "Palos" is comprised of three separate villages: Palos Heights, Palos Hills, and Palos Park, and these three towns slumber on the eastern border of the most underpopulated part of this very haunted territory. The district is bounded on its north end by phantom-riddled Archer Avenue, home to Chicago's most famous ghost, Resurrection Mary, an erstwhile South Side Polish girl who has, for more than seventy years, hitchhiked this old Indian road as far south as Willow Springs. Her stomping grounds are also home to the so-called Sobbing Woman of Archer Woods Cemetery, the gangland ghosts of Rico D's restaurant, an old Capone speakeasy, and the phantom automobiles tied in legend to the 1956 double-murder of little Barbara and Patricia Grimes, whose frozen bodies were eventually found at nearby Devil's Creek.

Archer Avenue was built in the early 1800s by Irish immigrants who settled in Chicago's Bridgeport neighborhood, near present-day Chinatown. The building of the road progressed in conjunction with a much larger, more significant project: the construction of the Illinois and Michigan Canal, a waterway that aimed to, at long last, connect by water the Chicago River and the Illinois River, thereby connecting the Great Lakes and the Mississippi River. Constructing the road over an old Indian trail that snaked southwest out of the city, immigrants worked under conditions that were often slave-like, going without pay or food—and sometimes without water—for days or weeks at a time. It is estimated that many hundreds of canal workers died along the canal route; indeed, one of Archer's most haunted sites is the churchyard of St. James, established near the Sag Bridge, which was founded to accommodate the bodies of the many dead canal workers.

The suffering of the Illinois and Michigan Canal workers certainly left a preternatural imprint on this atmospheric road, but other factors that have contributed to the haunting of Archer Avenue can also go a long way in explaining the haunting of the entire region south of it, most notably the presence of water.

Even before the building of the Illinois and Michigan Canal (and, with less fanfare, the Calumet-Sag Channel and the Illinois Sanitary and Ship Canal), the Des Plaines River flowed through this heavily-forested land, a landscape covered with lakes, ponds and sloughs. Though it was long-believed by many cultures that water keeps ghosts at bay, parapsychologists today contend that paranormal manifestations are actually encouraged by the presence of water, an excellent conductor for the electromagnetic energies that ghosts are thought to be.

Another contributor to the paranormality of this region may be the sheer under population of much of it. The Chicago area is rife with forest preserves, some of them even within the city limits, and these areas have long been notorious as hotbeds of supernatural phenomena. Why? Theories abound.

Of course, haunted houses most often harbor their ghosts in the attic or basement—areas with infrequent human visitors. Silly as it may seem, ghosts seem to prefer to "hide" from flesh-and-blood cohabiters rather than mix in with their everyday lives. It would follow, then, that forest preserves would be perfect habitats for Chicago ghosts with a distaste for the hustle and bustle of urban life.

Other theories, however, suggest that it is humans—and not haunts—that have infested Chicago's preserves. Some preserve visitors have attested to experiencing chanting and singing by unseen people; at times this chanting seems to be done by dozens of voices. Others have reported glimpsing apparitions of hooded or cloaked figures, including those seen at Red Gate Woods, along Archer Avenue, and at the notorious Bachelors Grove Cemetery, part of the Rubio Woods preserve, an overgrown woodland ossuary that remains one of the most haunted cemeteries in the nation. These audio and visual apparitions are often tied to the ritualistic activities that have been reported in Chicago-area preserves since at least the 1960s. Those who make the connection believe that these rituals, performed largely by amateurs, have conjured up nature or even evil spirits that their unskilled conjurers could bring forth, but not send back.

The little village of Palos Park is, today, pure woodland serenity, a pocket of humanity comprised largely of mid-twentieth century ranch houses bordering the great forested preserves of southwest Chicago. Residents commute to Chicago to work but thoroughly enjoy the riding stables, fishing holes, and hiking trails of their home village. Don't be fooled by this town's peaceful looks. The place holds a terrible secret indeed, if the legends of this town are true. For, at the foot of a hill on the grounds of Palos Park's unassuming, interactive "Children's Farm" (a petting zoo and interpretive center catering to school groups) is buried the head—and only the head—of a horrifying local maniac: the Demon Butcher of Palos Park.

Hermann Butcher was one of a number of small businessmen who migrated to the Palos region during the chaos of the Columbian Exposition of 1892, when the influx of visitors to Chicago—many of them eventually settling there—drove a significant section of the urban population to quieter realms outside the city limits. The town of Palos was originally dubbed "Trenton" at its founding in the 1830s; in 1850, the village was renamed by its postmaster, whose ancestor had sailed from Palos de Fronters with Christopher Columbus.

In the days of its establishment, Palos Park was a farming community in a region that had been alive with Indians and French explorers in the 1700s, but the building of the Wabash Railroad was the key to its survival, as it allowed non-farming residents with Chicago ties to establish homes in Palos beginning in the late 1800s.

Butcher, whose family name came from the long-held family business, was one of several German immigrants who set up butcher shops in Palos in the late-nineteenth century, but it wasn't long before he was the only butcher left in town. The significant depression that swept the United States in the 1890s did not miss Palos, and butchers here were pinned to the wall by the livestock shortage that accompanied it. Fortunately, Hermann Butcher was not only well-to-do, having enjoyed a thriving business in Chicago before his exodus, he was also well-connected to executives and managers at the best Chicago meat suppliers. Though he was forced, like his colleagues, to raise his prices, Butcher was able to remain in business.

No one knows whether Butcher's insanity stretched back further than his life in Palos, but what happened during his days here have made residents of Palos afraid to dig more deeply.

The atrocities began one afternoon when a large shipment of beef arrived at Butcher's shop. Like most butchers of the day, Hermann retained an apprentice who learned, at his side, the art and craft of butchering meat. Hermann was known in the village to drive his apprentice too hard. With a bad back and a sharp tongue, Butcher pawned off most of the daily workload onto his young charge, who bore the increasing burden with the patience of a saint. On this particular day, though, the shipment was larger than usual; Butcher pressed his apprentice to carry every parcel of it down to the basement meat locker, without a lick of assistance from the master. Unfortunately, a particularly heavy package of beef caused the young man to falter on the steep steps; he tumbled to the basement, breaking his neck with a fatal snap.

Butcher was horrified. He knew he had a reputation for working his apprentice into the ground and of disciplining him with his foul temper. Because of it, he had been on unfriendly terms with the boy's family for months. Would the apprentice's family think the boy's death had been Hermann's fault? That he had driven the boy too hard or, worse, in a flair of temper, pushed him down the stairs?

Strained by months of trying to keep his business afloat, Butcher wasn't willing to chance it. If he were accused of contributing in any way to his apprentice's death, who knew what could happen? And Butcher was sick of worrying and struggling. In a moment of desperation, Butcher stashed the apprentice's corpse behind the parcels of beef that the young man had just unloaded. He locked the freezer door and hoped for the best.

It wasn't long before the boy was missed, but inquiries as to his whereabouts were met by Butcher's own, feigned bewilderment and anger: I have no idea where he is, Hermann claimed, but when you find him, tell him to get into work immediately! Butcher claimed he hadn't seen the boy since he'd left work two days before; he suggested that the boy had been unhappy with the job and, perhaps, had decided to hop a Chicago-bound train to make his fortune in a more pleasing apprenticeship.

Despite his cool demeanor, the heat on Hermann increased as the week wore on. Adding stress was the always-dwindling meat supply. When fare for his customers was at an all-time low, Butcher took action. After closing up shop one evening, he made his way to the basement meat locker. Working by the light of a dim lantern, he carved up a portion of the apprentice's chilled left leg and packaged it in butcher paper. At home that night, Hermann roasted the leg meat and sat down to dinner. Sampling the morbid fare, he found it surprisingly similar to beef, but with an added sweetness that rendered it quite delectable.

Early the next morning, Butcher arrived at his shop and spent several hours butchering and displaying his gruesome offerings. When the first customers arrived, they were delighted to find the fine-looking cuts of meat and, in short time, every one was sold.

The next day, a nervous Butcher was waiting for the verdict on his grisly new supply. To his delight, the same customers returned, having found Hermann's "beef" scrumptious. Luckily, Butcher had carved up most of the apprentice's remaining corpse, so his customers went away happy again, but this couldn't last… or could it?

Butcher found himself newly perplexed. If he could not supply more of the flesh his customers craved, what would they do? Likely, try to find more of the strangely delicious beef themselves by contacting his suppliers. This simply couldn't be allowed. The supply would have to continue.

When the last scraps and bones had been sold, Butcher launched a fresh plan to protect his ever-floundering business. Each evening for weeks, he made his way out to the railroad yard and singled out a hungry-looking hobo. Promising food in exchange for some light labor, Hermann lured his victims back to his shop where he fed them a drugged dinner, washed down with potent schnapps, until they dozed off. When the unfortunate vagrant was suitably comatose, Butcher brought out his cleaver and hacked him up in his sleep, working late into the night to attractively arrange the cuts for sale the next day.

Soon, however, word spread through the hobo camp that something untoward was afoot; overnight, the camp emptied, and Butcher was again without meat for his shop.

By this time, Butcher had passed the point of no return. One by one, in the days that followed, the children of Palos began to go missing. Besides the hobos who could be plied with food and liquor, these little ones were all that Butcher, in his aged state, could handle.

Worse, with the first child's murder came even greater reviews of Butcher's products: Hermann's customers, of course, found the latest offerings the most succulent of all, so Butcher was insanely encouraged to provide more and more of the sickening stock.

Eventually, the locals began to suspect that one of their own villagers was behind the recent string of child abductions. Working with an assortment of tips—and driven by the hunches of the apprentice's family—a group of enraged villagers stormed Butcher's shop late one night, searching it from top to bottom and finding, in the basement meat locker, a shocking array of packaged body parts—and the remains of a seven-year-old child hanging from a meat hook.

Making their way to Butcher's home, the villagers forced entry and dragged Hermann out onto the lawn where they butchered him with his own cleaver. The final blow severed Butcher's head, which the people of Palos buried at Indian Hill across from Oak Hill Cemetery.

Today, Palos Park remains a uniquely peaceful suburb of Chicago, the greatest beneficiary of the preserves that surround it. Residents enjoy horseback riding, fishing, boating, and hiking in the beautiful woodlands that abut the village, and even the homes here nestle in lovely woodland settings. Still, at Oak Hill Cemetery, all is not at rest.

After the slaughter of Hermann Butcher and the burying of his head at Indian Hill, the murderer's headless remains were interred separately in a plot near the center of Oak Hill Cemetery, marked by a stone bearing only the name of "Butcher." But they haven't remained there. Residents of Palos Park tell of the body moving ever closer to the head. In fact, the grave has mysteriously moved twice already, from the center of the graveyard towards the road, to a plot near the pond, then to its current site along Southwest Highway itself. Is it only a matter of time before Butcher's body returns to its unbutchered state—rejoining its head across the road?

Of course, skeptics claim that the Butcher remains have been repeatedly moved by decidedly unsupernatural means. The water table at the cemetery is such, they say, that certain graves have become waterlogged over the years, forcing the caretakers to move them, sometimes more than once.

A visit to the Children's Farm on a warm summer afternoon seems to chase away all thoughts of ghosts. The air smells of hay and new-mown grass, and the sounds of young animals mingle with the laughter of children, visitors to the Farm enjoying its pleasant, natural surroundings.

Wandering away from the animals and the outbuildings, however, yields a distinctly different feeling, especially if one wanders toward Indian Hill.

The Mouths of Babes

John Wayne Gacy was not a textbook psychopath. There was nothing in his childhood psychologists could point to as the cause of his violence and rage. Even his family was baffled as to the reasons he became one of America's most sinister and notorious serial killers. To friends, neighbors, and business associates, he was the "man of the year." This, however, was his external self, the self he showed the world. Under his carefully-constructed façade was an evil inside that knew no control.

By all accounts, Gacy had a normal childhood. He grew up on Chicago's North Side in the 1940s and '50s. A self-described "sickly child," Gacy suffered from a head trauma that left him with an undetected blood clot on his brain which would cause him blackouts and fainting spells until he was in his teens. As a young adult, he suffered from a non-specific "heart ailment." As a child, John shied away from sports and physical activity, favoring instead activities his mother and sisters enjoyed, like baking and gardening. Gacy's father, a heavy drinker, would often publicly ridicule his son, calling him a sissy and a great disappointment. It was this abusive relationship with his father that Gacy often referenced as a formative experience in his life. John Sr. would often drink heavily in the basement before dinner only to come to the table and turn his family into targets of his verbal and physical abuse.

One of the great disappointments to Gacy's father was his son's inability to succeed in school. In his later years of high school, he blamed his failures on his fainting spells, and his grades dropped dramatically. After attending four different high schools in his senior year alone, Gacy finally dropped out. He moved out west to Las Vegas to seek his fortune only to find himself alone and miserable, hoping to return again to Chicago once he'd saved enough money.

Many rumors surround the work Gacy did in Las Vegas. That he worked as a janitor in a funeral home is certainly true, but many said he often slept in the empty caskets when he would get tired, a rumor he would always deny. He admitted that he'd lived in the funeral home but never slept in the caskets or did anything to violate the dead. What he was to do in his later life, however, fueled these rumors, and they became believable.

In 1962 Gacy returned to Chicago and enrolled in business college. It wasn't long before he had distinguished himself as a gifted salesman and began working for the Nunn Bush Shoe Company. He eventually moved south to Springfield to manage a men's clothing outlet store, and there he met his first wife,

Marlynn Myers, in 1964. Marlynn was from a rather prosperous family in Waterloo, Iowa. Her father owned a chain of Kentucky Fried Chicken restaurants, and Gacy set his sights on working his way into the family business.

One of the most startling qualities about Gacy, if not the most sinister, was his ability to ingratiate himself into the good opinion of the townspeople where he took up residence. He was very active in local politics and was a leading member of the Jaycees. He often sought leadership roles, whether as manager or recruiter, and he always craved the limelight. Affable and outgoing, this was what everyone remembered.

John and Marlynn Gacy moved with their newborn son to Waterloo, Iowa, where John was to manage one of his father-in-law's restaurants. Almost right away, he was seen as a pillar of the community, active in local affairs organizations; yet, when Gacy was arrested in 1968 for molesting a minor, not many seemed shocked. Rumors were circulating before the crime about John's penchant for young boys. He always seemed to be in the company of teenagers and was often organizing projects in which he could employ many local teens. Gacy was charged and convicted of sodomy after he'd forced himself on a young employee named Mark Miller. In his testimony, Miller claimed that Gacy had tricked him into being tied up and that Gacy had then violently raped him.

Gacy denied these charges. He claimed that Miller was a willing partner, and he later sent another boy, Dwight Andersson, to beat up Mark Miller.

During his trial, Gacy underwent a psychological evaluation. It was determined that he had an antisocial personality. He was sentenced to ten years in prison for sodomy, which was the maximum sentence he could receive in the state of Iowa. He spent eighteen months of his ten-year sentence at the Anamosa Prison before being paroled in 1970.

At age twenty-eight, Gacy was back in Chicago and living with his mother. His father had died while he was incarcerated, and his mother helped to support him until he decided to buy a house six months later. In 1971, Gacy bought a house at 8213 West Summerdale Avenue in then-unincorporated Chicago, on the far Northwest Side. His mother and sisters owned half the house, and he owned the other half. It was a nondescript ranch-style house on the quiet outskirts of Chicago. The community was very close, and most neighbors knew one another. They quickly embraced their new, very friendly neighbor.

Next door lived Edward and Lillie Grexa. They immediately took to Gacy, often having him over for cookouts, card games, and even Christmas dinner. They were charmed by the young man. In 1972, Gacy married again, this time a divorcée named Carole Huff, and he brought his new wife and her two daughters to live with him. The Gacy's appeared to enjoy the ideal household. Popular and accepted, the family often hosted elaborate themed parties and backyard barbeques, and Gacy even entertained at children's parties where he would dress up as "everyone's favorite clown, Pogo."

Lillie Grexa would often complain about a stench coming from the Gacy house. She told John that she thought an animal had died beneath the floorboards of the house, and that he should have that looked into. Gacy reassured Lillie that it was not a dead animal but most likely mold built up from an abundance of moisture under the house. This seemed to satisfy her curiosity and certainly did not keep the Grexas from the company of the Gacys.

Gacy himself set the year 1972 as the date of his first killing. On January 2, 1972, Gacy found a young Timmy McCoy at the Greyhound bus station in downtown Chicago, at Randolph and Dearborn. McCoy came home with Gacy, and the two had sex. Afterward, Gacy went to the kitchen, got a knife, and stabbed McCoy in the chest.

Thereafter, Gacy took to cruising the bus stations in downtown Chicago or headed over to Bughouse Square (Washington Park), a known hangout and pickup place for local gays. He became frustrated at home, eventually admitting to Carole that he preferred the company of young men to women.

In order to keep himself in the company of boys and young men, in 1974 Gacy started PDM (Painting, Decorating, and Maintenance), Inc. He employed a number of local high school boys, supposedly to keep costs low. It was also about this time that he began to set his sights on the political arena. Gacy threw himself into projects for his local Democratic committeeman. He was appointed Lighting Commissioner. He would have liked a life in politics, but public life, he found, could make things messy.

It was during a project at the Democratic headquarters that Gacy had hired a boy named Tony Antonucci. Antonucci claimed that Gacy had made advances toward him but had left him alone once Antonucci threatened to hit him with a chair. Gacy claimed it was all a joke and tried to laugh it off. Antonucci continued to work for him, and on a visit to Gacy's house, he claimed that Gacy had tricked him into being handcuffed. Antonucci made sure he was able to escape, got himself free, and then handcuffed Gacy in the scuffle. He made Gacy promise to leave him alone, and Antonucci left, not realizing how close he had come to his own death.

By 1976, Gacy's marriage had all but dissolved. His wife, Carole, claimed that they no longer had a sexual relationship, he was increasingly violent and suffered terrible, unpredictable mood swings, and she had discovered a number of hidden magazines in the house featuring naked young men and boys. It was at this time that Gacy confessed his love of boys to her, and she soon filed for divorce.

With Carole out of his house, there was nothing stopping Gacy from committing a string of the most atrocious murders in American history. Between 1972 and 1978, Gacy killed thirty-three young men and boys, some as young as fourteen, none older than twenty-one. Of those identified, a number of them had worked for Gacy at his contracting company, including John But-kovich. Johnny, as he was called, worked for Gacy in 1974, when he was seventeen years old. After a confrontation at Gacy's house, Johnny was seen driving home, and this was the last anyone saw of him.

Michael Bonnin was also seventeen. In 1976, he was on his way to meet his stepfather's brother and never made it. Gregory Godzik, also seventeen, worked for Gacy at PDM. The last anyone saw of Godzik was when he'd dropped off a date at her house. Gregory had a 1966 Pontiac, and this was all that was found of him. Billy Carroll was sixteen years old. Unlike the other boys, Billy had been in trouble with the law since he was a boy. He survived on the streets by setting up meetings between boys and adult men. On June 13, 1976, he left home and was never seen again.

John Szyc, nineteen, drove away from his home in his 1971 Plymouth Satellite and vanished. A little while later, the car was stopped for failing to pay at a gas station, but it was being driven by another boy. The boy told police they should talk to the man he lived with and he would sort it out; the man was John Wayne Gacy.

Gacy told the police that Szyc had sold him the car. If they had checked the car title, they would have seen that it was signed eighteen days after Szyc's disappearance. A similar fate befell Robert Gilroy, eighteen years old. Robert was going to meet friends when he disappeared. His father, a police sergeant, launched an investigation that yielded little.

In 1977, Gacy changed his routine slightly. He had picked up a man downtown, Jeffrey Rignall, twenty-seven years old. He asked him if he wanted to share a joint, then Gacy forced him into his car at gunpoint. Gacy repeatedly chloroformed Rignall and brought him to his house. There, for countless hours, Gacy tortured, raped, whipped, and chloroformed Rignall before returning him to the city to dump him in Lincoln Park. Rignall woke up in the park, very lucky to even be alive.

Finally, in 1978, Gacy's number came up. When a local boy, Robert Piest, fifteen, went missing from the pharmacy where he worked, the last person he was seen with was John Wayne Gacy. Witnesses claimed they saw Gacy talking to Piest about hiring him to work for his contracting company. Given his description and name, it was very soon that the police were knocking on Gacy's door.

Gacy told police he would meet them at the station and answer any questions they had about Piest. He went down and answered their questions, but they had nothing to hold him on, so they had to release him. Lieutenant Joseph Kozenczak had a bad feeling about Gacy, though, and put a twenty-four hour surveillance on him. Gacy went about town as though he had done nothing wrong, even picking up the officers' check in the diners where the police had followed him. Kozenczak was so sure about Gacy, though, that he was quickly given a search warrant to enter Gacy's house.

While he was away, police began to search Gacy's home. There they found some very bizarre collections: class rings, a police badge, nylon rope, a stained piece of carpet, pornography, boys' clothing, a pair of handcuffs, sexual devices, marijuana, various pills, a hypodermic needle, and a small vial. They impounded Gacy's vehicles; in the back of one were found pieces of hair that would later be determined to belong to Robert Piest. Police did make their way into Gacy's crawlspace, but were deterred by a rancid smell. Lime had been sprinkled in the crawlspace, but nothing else appeared to stand out.

This time when Gacy returned to the police station, he was not calm and collected. He was enraged and demanded a lawyer. Under the strain, with all his dark secrets on the verge of exposure, Gacy finally confessed—but to only one killing. He claimed he killed a young man in self-defense and then buried him under his garage. The police marked that, but they began digging in Gacy's crawlspace, and within fifteen minutes discovered the first of twenty-seven bodies.

On December 22, 1978, Gacy finally confessed to killing some thirty people and burying most of them under the house. He drew police a detailed map of where they should dig to find the bodies. He told the same story as Tony Antonucci had related: that he had tricked them into being handcuffed, that he had then raped them, and to muffle their terrified screams, stuff their socks or their underwear down their throats. One grizzly detail he offered police was that he kept some of the corpses under his bed for a few days before burying them. In all, police removed twenty-seven bodies from Gacy's crawlspace.

The body of Frank Wayne "Dale" Landingin had been discovered in the Des Plaines River a few weeks before. No one was looking for Gacy at the time, so no one was able to connect him to the crime right away. His driver's license was found among Gacy's collections. There were four more bodies that would be found in the Des Plaines River, but by February 1979, Robert Piest had still not been found. It was not until April 1979 that Piest's body washed up at the Dresden Dam in the Illinois River. The death toll was now up to thirty-three. This was the most heinous crime ever recorded in American history. Though other killers had claimed more victims, no greater number had ever been credited to one man.

In 1980, the trial of John Wayne Gacy was to begin. The prosecution called some one hundred witnesses to testify against Gacy. The defense, of course, clung to an insanity plea. While being interrogated, Gacy had created a split personality for himself. "There are four Johns," he explained. "John the contractor, John the clown, John the politician, and Jack Hanley." Jack Hanley was the killer. Often during questioning, he would tell police, "You'll have to ask Jack that." He seemed to be laying the groundwork for the insanity plea. The prosecution had been ready for this, and they called in a expert of their own. Gacy was determined fit for trial. He would answer for his crimes.

Gacy was convicted on thirty-three counts of murder and would receive the death penalty. He was sent to Menard Correctional Center in downstate Illinois. For fourteen years he remained there on death row before being transferred to Stateville Prison in Joliet, Illinois, to face execution. On May 10, 1994, at 12:48 A.M., John Wayne Gacy was given a lethal injection, and he died eighteen minutes later. His last words were reported to be, "Kiss my ass."

Gacy maintained he was innocent and that the twenty-seven bodies found in his basement were planted there by police, a rather remarkable claim in the face of such evidence. He also claimed he was not a homosexual. He seemed baffled by the fate he had constructed for himself. Most, however, were unmoved by tears of this clown.

In 1983, during his incarceration on death row at the Menard Correctional Center, John Wayne Gacy was stabbed by fellow inmate Henry Brisbon, the notorious "I-57 Killer," who in 1973 had, among other atrocities, dragged a woman from her car and forced her to walk naked through a barbed wire fence before shooting her in the vagina. The bizarre altercation found Gacy, unbelievably, at the mercy of someone at least as diabolical as himself.

Just before Christmas in 1978, Gacy had attended a party where fortunes were being read. Florence Branson, a renowned local psychic, was reading palms for the guests. Always one to join in the festivities, Gacy sat down opposite Branson. She noted that she was extremely disturbed by his aura and almost became physically sick when she tried to read his palm. Years later, when Branson read about his atrocities in the newspaper, she was not surprised at all.

While Gacy was being interrogated by police, he sent a neighbor over to check on his house. The neighbor got the key and put it in the lock at the back door. Before he could open it, he claimed he'd heard voices, a number of them, coming from inside the house. He described it as a moaning sound, though there didn't seem to be any particular place it was coming from—not upstairs nor down but as though the house itself was moaning. The neighbor later believed it was some sort of unrest contained inside the house. At the time, he'd passed it off as his mind "playing tricks on him" out of paranoia and fear.

The house Gacy lived in at 8213 West Summerdale Avenue became a place of pilgrimage to those seeking ghoulish thrills. After the police were finished with their search, nothing but rubble remained of the house, and in 1979 it was leveled. Still, the curious came. Strangely, nothing grew on the site of Gacy's house. It was as though the land itself was blighted by the evil it tried to contain. Skeptics claimed that the lime Gacy had used to cover his victims made the land inhospitable to vegetation; however, the entire property, down to several feet under the basement, had been dug up and hauled away during the investigation. All of the earth was new.

Eventually the property was purchased, and a new house has been built on the site, the address changed, and as though it has found some sense of renewal, there is vegetation and life growing on the land once again.

Photograph by the author

Site of the former home of John Wayne Gacy.

X.

Dunning is Haunted

The poor you always have with you.

—Matthew 26:11

*I*n my more than twenty years of official ghost hunting, fifteen years of research and writing, and a lifetime of interest in Chicago's paranormal history, no person, no event, no legend or lore has inspired the question of haunting more than the name of "Dunning." Yet, through all those years not a shred of a story had ever surfaced to suggest that any of the site's dreadful history still lives. That changed about a year ago.

I first saw the Dunning property when I was in the last years of elementary school, when my girlfriends and I would take the #80 Irving Park bus west from the North Center neighborhood where we lived to shop at the Harlem and Irving Plaza, affectionately

Photograph courtesy of Christine Zenino

**Chicago-Read Mental Health Center
sign on the Dunning property.**

known as "The HIP." By then the Dunning buildings were long gone, having been replaced by the Chicago-Read Mental Health Center. The "Read Center" had replaced the dreadful Dunning name for younger Chicagoans like me, who often heard of crazy people being locked up there for the rest of their lives.

The complex first opened as a poorhouse in 1851, where indigent individuals and families lived and worked an adjoining farm. It was during this early time that the Dunning name became affixed to the place, hailing from a local man's name on the nearby rail stop. The Dunning poor farm sprawled more than 150 acres that had been purchased from Peter Ludby, a farmer who had held the land via squatter's rights since 1839. Seven years after the poor farm opened, the Cook County Insane Asylum was completed on the acreage, directed by a Dr. D.B. Fonda. From the beginning, under-financing and overcrowding were problems.

Despite the inadequate resources, the need for a larger facility became increasingly apparent, and in 1871, the year of the Great Fire, a new structure was completed which was serving around six hundred patients by 1885. Two fires, in 1912 and 1923, destroyed great portions of the asylum structures and sent the city into a panic when, each time, a number of inmates escaped from the grounds. In 1912, a *Nashua Reporter* headline proclaimed the day after the fire: "Steward of Institution Struggles for Life with Crazy Man 75 feet in Air—Police Stops Scores From Suicide." In reality, a hospital employee who was trying to lead patients to safety from a burning building had to restrain one man who tried to run back inside. The two ended up in a skirmish near a bridge railing over a deep ditch. The "suicides" that were stopped were patients trying to escape upper rooms that were hopelessly aflame. In 1923, a second fire broke out which, according to the *Mansfield* (Ohio) *News*, "took a toll of at least seventeen lives and loosed a score of dangerously insane patients as a menace to the city."

New construction soon began to replace the destroyed infir-mary buildings, and in the summer of 1912 Cook County transferred the property and institution to the State of Illinois. The fearful name was officially changed to Chicago State Hospital, though, for Chicagoans, the "Dunning" moniker would always remain.

Richard Vachula lived much of his life in the Dunning area and wrote a great deal about the experience for internet research-ers. Some of his work may still be found at AbandonedAsylum. com, where I found his work with the help of Daniel Pogorzelski of the Jefferson Park Historical Society. Vachula writes about the welcome change that came in the 1950s when electro-shock therapy (ECT) was largely replaced by chemotherapy at Dunning:

> *When ECT was administered to the patients, neigh-bors along Narragansett (Avenue) could hear loud screams and pleas for mercy. I can recall as a youngster while riding my bicycle along Narragansett and hearing these cacophonous sounds. It was enough to unnerve anybody.*

Life in the Dunning neighborhood meant days and nights perpetually undermined by a constant, though largely unfounded, fear of patient escape. As Vichula recalls:

> *Besides the unrelenting screams, there always ex-cited a fear among the neighborhood surrounding CSH (Chicago State Hospital) that an inmate would escape at night, break into one's home, and strangle someone in their bed. People living around CSH locked their doors, slept with a pipe or baseball bat by their beds, or even kept a gun or knife in reaching distance. Their irrational fear caused strange behavior.*

There was the occasional patient who did manage escape, sometimes regularly, like the so-called "Wolfman" who would flee to nearby Mount Olive Cemetery during full moons and howl until retrieved by security and police. Others' attempts were not so easily rectified, like that of a woman who became impaled on the eight-foot hospital fence during a 1951 bid at freedom.

In the late 1980s, Pontarelli, a prolific Chicago real estate developer, purchased the land with the intention of building a residential community on the old Dunning grounds. When digging began, workers shocked the boss with the news that skeletal remains were being uncovered, and in astonishing numbers. According to the *Chicago Tribune* of July 9, 1990:

> *Among them was the mummified torso of a man so well preserved that he showed the handlebar mustache and mutton-chop sideburns of the 1890s. There were other remains: several baskets of bones, perhaps representing the bodies of several dozen people...*

Archaeologists at Loyola University were hired to excavate, and many university students volunteered to assist in the painstaking process. It was revealed that three separate cemeteries had occupied the land, containing unclaimed victims from the Great Fire, orphaned children, penniless veterans of the Civil War, the dead of the poor farm, and Dunning inmates who had perished

Photograph by the author

Read-Dunning Memorial Park at sunset.

Photograph courtesy of Christine Zenino

View of Read-Dunning Memorial Park

as patients. Also presumably among them were the bodies from the potter's field at the original City Cemetery in Lincoln Park, which were reportedly moved to the poor farm after the cemetery was closed and which are likely included among the "Itinerant Poor" memorialized at the new Read-Dunning Memorial Park. The park was built on a three-acre tract of land set aside for re-interment of the remains found at the Dunning site, and today the site is complete, its final design a snaking pathway connected by seven concrete circles. At its dedication on December 18, 2001, the remains of the 182 disturbed graves were reburied in an official memorial service to dedicate the park. There was much talk that day of the unfortunate of Dunning finally being at peace. But perhaps not all have found the rest they deserve.

I finally heard of the haunting of the Dunning property about a year ago at a meeting of the Jefferson Park Historical Society. I had been invited to speak there by Daniel Pogorzelski, vice president of the society, and during the question and answer session, someone asked if I knew of any hauntings at the nearby Dunning site. I admitted that I had searched in vain for years for stories of

Photograph courtesy of Christine Zenino

**Memorial to the Insane Asylum dead,
Read-Dunning Memorial Park.**

phenomena there, and I jokingly pleaded for someone to come forward with even a ghostly rumor of the place.

After the presentation, I was approached by a half-dozen members who, in fact, had some amazing stories to tell of the old asylum grounds. I went into the night blissful, entranced, and more than a little unnerved.

As part of the development of the Dunning property, Wright Community College, previously housed in an early-twentieth-century building, designed a new, relatively sprawling modern campus, centered around a pyramidal structure housing faculty offices, the campus library, and computer labs. Tales of the paranormal are rife among the Mexican and Polish-American cleaning staff at the college, who have witnessed everything from lights turning on and off to full-scale apparitions of figures in nineteenth-century clothing.

Pogorzelski told me of a woman he knows, an immigrant from Ireland, who refuses to shop at the Jewel food store in Dunning Square Mall because it was built on the asylum property and is rumored to be haunted. She deliberately shops across the street, at the Polish market, Wally's, though she is one of the only non-Poles who patronizes the place.

Most unsettling are the encounters that reportedly continue at the local ward office on Irving Park Road, where employees have seen a grey-haired elderly woman in a hospital gown.

One Chicago-area investigator held a "ghost box" session at the Read-Dunning Memorial Park, attempting to communicate in real time with the ghosts of the vanquished asylum. A ghost box is a popular tool used by increasing numbers of researchers to collect what many believe to be spirit voices. A ghost box is simply a radio that has been built—or adjusted—to consistently and quickly scan through the AM or FM band. Box enthusiasts believe that the resulting indecipherable sounds provide spirits

Photograph courtesy of Christine Zenino

Rusting playground equipment outside a former children's facility on the Dunning property.

with vocal bytes from which they can create words to answer our questions. At Dunning, this particular researcher picked up some astounding samples (later posted on YouTube), including "All of us are dead," "I'm backwards," "Children bike on our heads," and "You're sitting on our carcasses."

XI.

Coming Apart

Dreams in the dusk,
Only dreams closing the day
And with the day's close going back
To the gray things, the dark things,
The far, deep things of dreamland.

—Carl Sandburg
Chicago Poems

For the past decade in the cornfields about forty miles south of Chicago, people have sought out one of the most notoriously haunted sites in the region. Once the largest state-run mental health facility in Illinois, Manteno State Hospital, or Diversitech, is now just a smattering of ramshackle remains. While all is now seemingly abandoned, razed or rehabbed, voices—very real ones—can still be heard in the halls and subterranean tunnels of this legendary insitution.

Begun in 1929, the Manteno State Hospital was designed to house the patients that facilities in Elgin and neighboring Kankakee could not accommodate. The new institution grew to one thousand acres, with one hundred buildings on its grounds. MSH, like most state asylums, was quiet on the outside, but also like most asylums, the outside belied a turbulent and sometimes violent life on the inside. From 1929 onward, the patient numbers at MSH grew steadily until 1954 when the hospital reached its largest population. At its founding, Manteno housed about a thousand patients. Between 1935 and 1936, the patient population doubled from 1309 to 3186 residents. By 1954, there were a staggering 8100 residents.

MSH was supposed to be a different kind of "asylum." It was designed as a grouping of smaller, one to two storey buildings rather than a towering institution. Each building was to be named for a progressive forerunner in the field of psychiatric care and research. Sigmund Freud, for example, lent his name to the dining hall; one of the wards housing female patients was named for Dorothea Dix. The physical design echoed the mission of Manteno: to be progressive in the treatment of the mentally ill, most notably, that patients could be rehabilitated through work. Accordingly, MSH had a working farm, a sewage treatment facility and its own power plant. For a decade, Manteno's functioning all seemed well.

In 1939, disaster struck. On July 9, a man whose entire contact at the hospital consisted of moving between the building in which he slept and the building in which he ate, came down with a mysterious fever of 104 degrees. Thinking he had tuberculosis, the staff began a series of tests. Two days later he was diagnosed with typhoid. Five days after that, he was dead. Another fifty-nine deaths would amount to a typhoid epidemic.

Despite its progressive claims, Manteno's state hospital was similar to most, if not all, of the state-run facilities in their treatment of the mentally ill. Well into the 1970s patients were still given hydrotherapy and subjected to sensory deprivation chairs or chambers, twirling chairs, and needle cabinets. Needle cabinets were steel cabinets in which the patients were placed and a nurse would administer needles filled with water that would be inserted directly under the skin. Straight jackets were used, as well as shackles. In later years, as technology advanced, alternatives included shock treatments with the use of insulin, the use of fever cabinets, electroshock therapy and prefrontal lobotomies. If a cure was unavailable, then control was the next best thing. The goal for most hospitals of this kind was to make the patient docile.

MSH had its own staff of physicians, surgeons, dentists, psychiatrists, nurses and aides. Surgery was performed on the grounds, whether lobotomies (the removal of the frontal lobe of the brain, usually by either drilling holes in the forehead above the eyes, or through the eye sockets), hysterectomies (the removal of the uterus), exploratory laparotomies (the cutting into the wall of the abdomen, usually in the groin area), and ileostomies (the surgical creation of an artificial canal for the drainage of the small intestine, permanent and irreversible). In 1941, each of these methods of "treatment" was commonplace. Agony was common, recovery rare. Because of the nature of mental illness, the low rate of recovery and release, and the abandonment of patients by their families, most patients, at death, were buried by the hospital. MSH had designated its own cemetery and buried fatalities in small graves marked with numbers. Today, this cemetery is so obscured by time, it is impossible to find. It does not appear on any of the original plans for the facility. Those who died here remained anonymous, nearly as anonymous as they were while alive, as many family members relinquished all rights to their patient-relatives, to divorce themselves from the stigma of mentally ill relations. There is no knowing how many are anonymously buried on the grounds.

An unforeseen addition to the population of the Manteno State Hospital was in the area of the criminally insane. Those who were convicted of violent crimes or felonies and were classified as criminal "by reason of mental illness or defect" were sent to Manteno, though MSH had no facility for dangerous patients. As a result the community was kept on constant alert due to frequent escapes. In 1977, a special ward was built for patients classified as "mittimus" (referring to their prison sentencing).

By 1983 the decision was made to close the Manteno State Hospital. Much of the grounds were given to establish a veteran's hospital, and within two years, the Manteno State Hospital was closed. A walk in the remaining wards seems like everything was left where it was, and that everyone just walked away. Beds—now empty—still stand at the ready, not even stripped of their linen. Gurneys are rusted to their spots in the halls. The main rooms overlook the decay of the grounds through large picture windows.

Today, Diversitech (as MSH is known locally) is a very different place. Of the one hundred buildings, many have either been converted for use by the veteran's hospital or have been demolished to make way for an industrial park and housing development. Thrill seekers and local teenagers still swarm the grounds after dark, and each has a story to tell of their experiences at the so-called haunted hospital. The underground tunnels at Manteno, in particular, have become places of pilgrimage to those seeking proof of the paranormal residents believed to remain here, as only two of the original ward buildings remain.

Driving up the winding road of the park-like campus, an eerie silence falls all around. It feels peaceful, like the entire place is sleeping. The narrow, tree-lined road, after a half mile, turns into a public square, dominated by the stately administration building, which now houses a commercial bank.

In early evening of an overcast day, the grounds sprawling from this square lend themselves to the stories. Decay has set in. Broken windows hide shadows inside. What the bulldozers won't do, time will. It seems as though at any minute, all around will come crumbling down.

At Manteno yet today, stories abound of apparitions, disembodied voices and poltergeist activity. Many EVP (electronic voice phenomenon) recordings have captured the voice of a nurse, seemingly over a PA system, paging either doctors or patients. Her calls have been heard by the naked ear as well, along with the voices of children. In the tunnels beneath the wards, it is not uncommon for visitors to feel the small hand of a child in theirs.

Of the countless photos that have been taken of the Manteno grounds since its abandonment, those of "Gennie's Message" are probably the most numerous. Gennie Pilarski was sent to MSH by her parents in 1944 when she was a young woman. It's believed today that she suffered from bipolar disorder, but nearly two hundred electroshock treatments, a lobotomy, and countless sessions of hydrotherapy left her, according to reports, incapable of human interaction or self-determination. At some point after the closing of the hospital, a sympathizer of Gennie's wrote excerpts from her patient records over the walls of one of the bathrooms in memory of the tortures patients endured here. Covering the room, from floor to ceiling and the hydrotherapy tubs, both inside and out, are large black letters detailing her life of misery at the infamous MSH. Gennie died in a nursing facility in 1998.

XII.

The Art of Haunting

An artist must take care not to trap his soul in the canvas.

—Dena Groquet

One of the most interesting investigations I have ever done took place at the Art Institute of Chicago in 2008. I had been contacted by a graduate student at the School of the Art Institute who had become intrigued by a fascinating question: Do artists, with all of the emotion invested in their pieces, somehow "haunt" their works?

A colleague and I met with Thomas Gokey in his studio space at the school and talked at length about the themes involved in his work, the relationships between the mind and paranormal activity, and the artists who inspired Gokey to start thinking about some amazing possibilities.

A few weeks later, Gokey had obtained permission for us to "investigate" a number of pieces in the institute's collection, and we met one afternoon to proceed with the project.

We were a strange sight in the galleries that day, holding EM meters and tape recorders to paintings, sculptures, and ancient artifacts. Everywhere we went, security guards were more than a little concerned about our intentions. Our explanations didn't do much to ease them. The awkward feelings, however, were well worth the experience, and we did experience several incidents that made us wonder.

The first work investigated was a painting by Jackson Pollock entitled *Greyed Rainbow* which was completed in 1953, just a few years before his death. Pollack, of course, had been one of the major influences in the abstract expressionist movement, and his drip painting or splatter painting, as most describe it, is one of the most recognizable styles of the twentieth century. A man of

Photograph courtesy of Thomas Gokey

**Checking for EMF fluctuations
at Jackson Pollock's *Greyed Rainbow***

volatile temperament and a voracious alcoholic, Pollack's paint-ings seemed to reflect the often chaotic nature of his personal life, and Gokey wondered if there may have been some paranomal-ity involved in his work, reminiscent of the almost spasmodic physical phenomena associated with poltergeist cases, in which a troubled mind is thought to unconsciously influence the move-ment of objects and other activity. We took temperature readings around the painting and scanned the area to find any fluctuations in the electromagnetic (EM) fields around the piece, but nothing out of the ordinary was found, at least through our preliminary investigation.

The second piece on the roster was located in the Spanjer Gallery, a collection of artifacts from the ancient Americas and American Indian art. The initial object of our attention was a piece called *The Storyteller*, a figure from the West Mexican State of Jalisco, c. 100-800 A.D. Though we asked a number of questions at the display case, hoping to capture some audible answers via electronic voice phenomenon (EVP, or the electronic recording of spirit voices), none came. As we said goodbye and thank you to

Photograph courtesy of Thomas Gokey

We try to get the figure of *The Storyteller* to talk to us via EVP.

whoever might be listening, however, our EM meter spiked twice, a possible indication of paranormal activity.

In the same gallery, mural fragments from the Teotihuacan culture (c. 300-750 A.D.) and a limestone stele seemed to host no unusual activity, so we moved our investigation back to modern times—and interesting results.

Our next stop was an Ad Rheinhardt work simply entitled *Abstract Painting,* one of the artist's so-called "black paintings" that he produced in the 1960s, not long before his death. A sudden drop in temperature of approximately fifteen degrees occurred at one point in our monitoring, and there was an EM spike after we said goodbye, identical to our experience in the earlier gallery.

Without question, the most provocative part of our investigation was that of Carl Andre's *Steel Aluminum Plain,* completed in 1969, a pattern of floor tiles typical of the artist's work. Andre's work has received much acclaim, but the most talked-about aspect of his life is not his art but an incident that occurred in his personal life.

Photograph courtesy of Thomas Gokey

Collecting EVP at Ad Rheinhardt's *Abstract Painting*

Photograph courtesy of Thomas Gokey

Recording temperature and EVP at Carl Andre's *Steel Aluminum Plain*

Andre met artist Ana Mendieta at a New York City gallery in 1979, and the two married in 1985. Tragically, Mendieta fell from Andre's thirty-fourth storey apartment that same year, and her husband was charged with second-degree murder. Andre declined a jury trial, and in 1988 he was acquitted of all charges by the judge of the case. Controversy still rages, however, regarding Mendieta's death, and Gokey wondered if we could tap into the truth by channeling the artist—still living—by approaching one of his works.

Andre encourages the trampling of his floor-level works by gallery-goers, and so I walked onto *Steel Aluminum Plain* with my EM meter and recorder to talk to the man himself and to ask him what had happened that fateful day at his New York apartment. The moment I squatted down to get closer, before I could ask for the truth, my EM meter spiked and the recorder shut itself off.

XIII.

Unmentionables

Yet we have gone on living;
Living and partly living.

—T.S. Eliot
Murder in the Cathedral

*T*hroughout my years of writing and lecturing on Chicago's so-called haunted history, readers and audience members know that I have tried to avoid addressing the subject of recent hauntings. Still, I am asked always about the tragedies of recent times—about whether paranormal residue remains at the scenes of yesterday morning's headlines. In the past few weeks, in this summer of 2009, I've been asked a hundred times about the recent discoveries at Burr Oak Cemetery—the south suburban burial ground where, it was recently revealed, an unknown number of bodies were dug up over many years, their remains all but discarded in a rear area of the cemetery so that the graves might be illegally resold. What I can say about Burr Oak is that the living were—and are—totally invested in those who repose there, wherever their physical remains are eventually found, secured, and laid to real rest. As for hauntings, I would imagine that there is restless activity befitting the atrocity of the discovery. I would also imagine that, after much anguish and a lot of labor to put it right, the dead of Burr Oak will be at peace.

For better or worse, I'm going to end this volume—and this chapter in my writing life—with some insight, at last, into the worst of the events I've avoided. I hope that these stories hurt no one. They aren't meant to. I don't know how these things happen, or even if they really do. But I know that, for whatever reason—and by whatever mechanism—they are real, very real, in some wondrous way. Just as the stories they tell—and the people we've lost—are always, always with us, even if we can't see them anymore.

On January 8, 1993, the owners and five employees of a Brown's Chicken Restaurant at 168 West Northwest Highway in suburban Palatine were brutally murdered by a former employee and his high school buddy. Juan Luna and James Degorski, just eighteen and twenty years old, entered the restaurant a short while before closing time, sat down and ate, and then cut one of the owner's throats, stabbed one of the employees, herded the rest of the victims into the walk-in cooler, and shot them with twenty rounds of a .38 caliber pistol. After stealing $1800 from the safe and trying to mop up the blood, the intruders turned off the lights and went silently into the snow outside. It wasn't until around six hours later that police finally heeded the many frantic phone calls from the victims' family members and arrived at the scene of the ghastly event.

Not long after what became known as "The Brown's Chicken Massacre" or "The Palatine Chicken Murders," the restaurant was closed; later, a dry cleaning shop moved in. The new tenants reportedly were plagued by all manner of paranormal phenomena, including cold spots, sounds of gunfire, screaming and crying, and an overwhelming feeling of sadness. After just a few years in business, the dry cleaners closed; two years later, in 2001, the building was demolished. The site was repaved and disappeared into the parking lot of the adjacent strip mall, but unusual phenomena continued. Cars parked within the old perimeter of the building reportedly stalled or would not start—until they were towed out of the invisible boundaries. Screams and sounds of weeping continued, as well as reports of shadowy figures on the site.

Reports of the phenomena continued until the spring of 2002, when Degorski's former girlfriend came forward to tell the story she'd kept in her heart for nearly a decade. Luna went to trial in 2007 and was convicted of all seven murders, sentenced to life in prison; Degorski's trial was set to begin in August of 2009. The murder site, they say, is quiet.

◆

On the morning of October 25, 1995, seven high school students were killed on their way to school when their school bus failed to clear the tracks at a rail crossing in suburban Fox River Grove. The driver was unaware that the back of the bus had not cleared the tracks, but because of a red light at the highway just beyond the crossing, the driver would regardless have been unable to move out of harm's way without passing through the red light. In the months before the tragedy, officials had reportedly received numerous complaints from the public about the dangerous timing between the warnings provided by the signals, and citizens later told of situations with vehicles unable to clear the tracks in a timely manner.

As a result of the accident, many such "interconnected" timing systems were reassessed and improved. Interestingly, since the tragedy, a recurring phenomenon has been said to occur at the crossing site. Local lore claims that if your car stalls on the tracks (or if you deliberately drive onto the tracks and shift into neutral), your vehicle will be pushed to safety by unseen hands—presumably those of the accident victims—and that the handprints of these invisible helpers may be seen in the dust on the backs of the cars. This phenomenon, commonly reported at such sites, was supposedly first experienced after a tragic school bus accident in San Antonio in the 1940s (see "The Ghastly Outdoors").

In Fox River Grove, ghostly attendants—if they exist—have not been enough. On the anniversary date of the tragedy, in 2006, a teenager crossing through the same intersection on his bicycle was fatally struck, shocking the entire metropolitan area, and bewildering a town still reeling from the events of eleven years past.

◆

The Epitome Chicago nightclub and its upstairs dance area, E2, combined to form one of the hottest nightclubs in Chicago, catering almost exclusively to the African American community. On Monday, February 17, 2003, twenty-one people were killed and scores injured when a security guard used pepper spray to break up a fight among patrons. At the time, the September 11 attacks and the 2001 Anthrax scare were fresh on the minds of Americans, and fearful nightclubbers rushed the exits.

Similarities to the Iroqouis tragedy could not be ignored: questions of emergency exits chained shut to prevent entry by non-paying patrons; inward-opening doors; a single known exit stairwell down which tumbled body after body on top of others below, pushed in the panic and trampled before security guards could help them up. More than fifteen hundred rushed to reach safety; almost two dozen never did. An inadequately trained staff, building code violations, and overcrowding, the list of problems at E2 cited by the press, the city, the county, and, indeed, the world weirdly echoes those behind the Iroqouis disaster more than a century earlier.

Photograph by the author

Former site of the Epitome / E2 Nightclub.

In November of 2008, Cook County prosecutors formally dropped their charges of involuntary manslaughter against E2 nightclub owner, Dwain Kyles. An order had been issued before the disaster requiring the club to close due to code violations, but the order was found to be inadmissible in Kyles' trial.

After the disaster, in the weeks and months—and years—that followed, the odd paranormal investigator made the edgy trek to the E2 site at 2347 South Michigan Avenue, hoping for a photograph, a voice, a fluctuation or two on the EM scale that might bear up as evidence that the dead are still here in some physical way. Though I've heard of no such evidence, rumors occasionally surface of music booming in the wee hours from behind the bolted doors and of screams that still echo along this somehow desolate block.

On our tours, our guides are trained to build a hopeful picture from the debris of these disasters. Our nightly visit to the site of the Iroqouis inferno, for example, finds us praising the sweeping changes in building safety that occurred after the fire. In reality, we continue to be haunted because little really changes.

What are the ghosts trying to tell us? Whatever their meaning, their messages fall, again and again, to deaf ears.

Just four months after the E2 nightclub disaster, around one hundred people were gathered for a summer party in the lively Chicago neighborhood of Lakeview, not far from Wrigley Field, celebrating on the top two floors of a typical three-flat residence. Dozens of revelers were enjoying the evening breezes on the wooden back porches of the two apartments when, sometime after midnight, the splintering of boards was heard, and the top porch gave way, collapsing on top of the porch below before the entire structure crashed into the basement of the building.

When firefighters arrived on the scene, they found, according to Chicago Fire Commissioner James Joyce, "(chaos)... people screaming and crying in the alley." Firefighters and paramedics took just an estimated ten minutes to remove the victims, yet

Photograph by the author

**The new, *steel* structure at the site of the 2003 porch collapse.
Signs on the stairs now say, "No parties or gatherings."**

thirteen people were crushed or asphyxiated in the collapse and more than fifty injured.

As is almost typical in such cases, passers-by in the days that followed observed figures standing or crouching in the alley behind the building who would disappear when approached. The sound of the many victims at the moment of the collapse was also reported by some in the weeks that followed—a cry of uncertainty and shock that some, at the time of the accident, mistook for a whoop of celebration.

After the collapse, a sweeping campaign ensued to crack down on unsafe porches, and thousands were reportedly inspected in the months after the horrific event, but after the initial push, the city simply was not able to be very proactive with ongoing efforts and today reportedly relies on 311 (non-emergency city hotline) calls from neighbors to track down dangerous structures and get them on the inspection list.

Accidents and injuries have continued to dot the headlines, and in June 2005, a nine-year-old South Side Chicago girl died when a porch railing gave way during a game of tag; in May 2009, two young people were talking on a back porch when the railing broke open and the two fell twenty feet to the alley beneath, one suffering a neck fracture, the other head injuries.

Reportedly, unusual phenomena persists at the site of the 2003 collapse.

In Chicago, then, as elsewhere, many so-called "accidents" are not really accidents at all. They are what happens when there are too many factors at play, too many unknowns, not enough money, manpower, or will to make sure they don't. And tragedies are tragedies because they didn't have to happen. Greed is often the dynamo in both cases, and in both cases unrest almost always lingers. The ghost stories symbolize it, even if you don't believe them.

But sometimes accidents are just that and nothing more. They seem to happen to make us cherish what we are, how wonderful life is, to tell us that it must—absolutely must—go on.

In May 2003, a group of high school students from the Cor Jesu Academy in St. Louis were on a glorious field trip to Chicago. It was a bustling Saturday afternoon at the popular Museum of Science and Industry in Jackson Park. A lovely, kind, vivacious seventeen-year-old girl was walking down one of the museum's open stairwells from the third floor with her classmates when she attempted to slide down the stair railing sideways. According to witnesses, she misjudged the distance, lost her balance, and fell four stories to the basement floor below, perishing almost instantly.

Security guards told me a year later, "We still see her. She's beautiful. She's smiling."

AFTERWORD

My own true ghost story didn't end when my dad passed away. In fact a few days after the funeral, my brother came home from a meeting and was getting ready to go up to bed when a thunderous banging began on the back porch door, as if someone was desperately trying to get in. The door shook as though it would become unhinged, yet no one was there. The door was paned in glass and, clearly, no one stood beyond. The banging went on for nearly fifteen minutes while our mom and I slept soundly just upstairs, unmoved.

In the weeks that followed, we became gradually unglued by all manner of phenomena: footsteps on the stairs, as we'd heard when we were children, and voices in the next room that would dissipate when we entered. One afternoon, we heard my electronic keyboard playing upstairs; yet when we entered my bedroom, it was under the bed, as it always was, with no batteries installed. As time progressed, the activity increased, until each evening was punctuated by loud hammering from the basement. One Friday night, about two months after my dad had died, my mom and I were watching television in the front room. My brother and I were attending college in the western suburbs, and I had elected to come home that night while my brother stayed at school. At about nine o'clock he called us and was quite homesick. We were all still very taken with my father's recent passing, and we had been clinging to each other through those first weeks. That night, on the phone, we talked for many minutes. He said he wished he'd come home. We said the same.

About ten minutes after the phone call ended, my mom and I heard the most incredible sequence of sounds from the front hall: keys turning in the locks, the noisy old front door opening and closing behind itself, the locks turning again, and the chain sliding across the latch. We turned to each other while we heard the distinct sound of the interior door brush against the foyer carpet. I opened my mouth to say, "Adalbert is home," but the words caught in my throat. My brother and I had spoken on the phone just ten minutes before. In those days before cell phones, he was forty miles away.

There was no doubt in either of our minds that someone had come in the front door, but it was impossible. We were sitting in full view of it. The experience was so real that we became immediately convinced that an intruder had gone upstairs without us seeing. My first instinct was to run, to go next door and call 911. My mom, ever sensible, made another, whispered suggestion. "Let's wait at the foot of the stairs," she said, "and listen." Our house was nearly a century old, and she was right. If someone upstairs took a breath, a floorboard would creak. We would know.

So we stood there, at the base of that staircase our ghost had traversed each night when I was a girl, and we held our breath, and we listened. Not fifteen seconds later, a wondrous thing happened. We heard the sound, not of a creaking floorboard, but of a mountain of boxes tumbling down. A moment later, we were finally next door, calling the police.

The neighborhood, then, was absolutely serene, and five minutes after our call six squad cars arrived on the scene. My mom and I stood outside on the neighbors' steps, freezing in the February night, while twelve officers searched the house, two by two. We were utterly certain that, any moment, one would come out with our invader in cuffs.

But none did.

A search from attic to basement by six pair of Chicago's Finest yielded no one, and nothing had been upset despite the incredible sounds we had heard.

In the end, the last pair of officers left, asking us if we'd be okay. My mom and I, trying to be tough, said yes. When they walked down the stairs, I heard one say to the other, "Must be ghosts."

The next day, I called our parish office and asked to speak to a priest about a personal matter. I was put in touch with a newly ordained, who had received his commission just the summer before. When I stammeringly told him what the problem was, he said, "Don't be embarrassed. It happens all the time."

That young priest came to dinner that winter Friday night. My mom made her specialty, Wiener Schnitzel, with all the trimmings. We laid the table in the beautiful dining room my great Uncle Andrew had built, with the built-in oak china cabinet, where we had celebrated so many happy times.

We had to stop the meal halfway because of the footsteps upstairs.

The priest went to the foyer and retrieved his prayer book. He stood and made the Sign of the Cross. "Sustain our hearts," he began, "and make us glad and grateful." We left the festive table, and we followed him through the house as he blessed each room. There was a different prayer for each one, I remember, and we heard rumblings as we went. There was the prayer for the kitchen, where we asked to "be thankful for our daily bread." There was the prayer for the bedrooms, in which we asked for the grace "to keep watch with Christ." There was even a prayer for the bathroom, where we prayed "to be refreshed in mind in spirit."

When we had finished, we returned to the dining room. We stood around the table, where twelve years later we would toast my father's memory, after my wedding, with family and friends bursting the house and champagne everywhere. "Be our shelter, Lord, when we are at home," he said, "our companion when we are away, and our welcome guest when we return."

Everyone sat down again, and I went to the kitchen and poured the coffee.

All has been quiet in the house on Bell Avenue since that night more than twenty years ago. My mom has her routine. She lays out her cereal bowl at night, puts the coffee in the filter, and goes up to the pile of books on her nightstand. A few blocks away, I'm putting my daughters in bed, and a few blocks the other way, my brother and his wife are getting ready for a well-deserved rest. There are no bumps in the night anymore, no steps on the stairs, no voices in the next room.

All of us, though, are more haunted than ever. Like those left behind after every story in this book, I know we always we will be.

SELECT BIBLIOGRAPHY
AND RECOMMENDED READING

Allegrini, Robert V. *Chicago's Grand Hotels.* Arcadia Publishing, 2005.

Asfar, Dan. *Haunted Highways.* Lone Pine Publishing, 2003.

Baatz, Simon. *For the Thrill of It: Leopold, Loeb, and the Murder That Shocked Jazz Age Chicago.* Harper Perennial, 2009.

Barton, Blanche. *The Secret Life of a Satanist.* Feral House, 1992.

Belanger, Jeff. *Communicating With the Dead.* Career Press, 2008.

Bielski, Ursula. *Chicago Haunts: Ghostlore of the Windy City.* Thunder Bay Press, 2009.

———. *More Chicago Haunts: Scenes from Myth and Memory.* Thunder Bay Press, 2008.

Bradley, Mickey, and Dan Gordon. *Haunted Baseball: Ghosts, Curses, Legends & Eerie Events.* The Lyons Press, 2007.

Breo, Dennis L. *The Crime of the Century* (on the Richard Speck Murders). Bantam, 1993.

Clarke, Lee. *Worst Cases: Terror and Catastrophe in the Popular Imagination.* University Of Chicago Press, 2005.

Clearfield, Dylan. *Chicagoland Ghosts.* Thunder Bay Press, 1997.

Cochrane, Hugh. F. *Gateway to Obllivion: The Great Lakes Bermuda Triangle.* Doubleday, 1980.

Condit, Carl W. *The Chicago School of Architecture: A History of Commercial and Public Building in Chicago, 1875-1925.* University Of Chicago Press, 1998.

Cowan, David. *Great Chicago Fires.* Lake Claremont Press, 2001.

Crowe, Richard T. *Chicago Street Guide to the Supernatural.* Carolando Press, 2000.

Eghigian, Mars, Jr. *After Capone: The Life And World Of Chicago Mob Boss Frank "the Enforcer" Nitti.* Cumberland House Publishing, 2006.

Gallery, Daniel V. *Twenty Million Tons Under the Sea: The Daring Capture of the U-505 .* Bluejacket Books, 2001.

Goebeler, Hans, and John Vanzo. *Steel Boat Iron Hearts: The Wartime Saga of Hans Goebeler and U-505.* Savas Beatie, 2008.

Gourley, Jay. *The Great Lakes Triangle.* Fawcett, 1977.

Guiley, Rosemary Ellen. *The Encyclopedia of Ghosts and Spirits.* Facts on File, 1992.

Hanson, George. *The Trickster and the Paranormal.* Xlibris, 2001.

Hatch, Anthony P. *Tinder Box: the Iroqouis Theater Disaster, 1903.* Academy Chicago Publishers, 2003.

Henderson Floyd, Margaret. *Henry Hobson Richardson: A Genius for Architecture.* Monacelli, 1997.

Holli, Melvin G., and Peter D. Jones. *Ethnic Chicago: A Multicultural Portrait.* William B. Eerdmans Publishing Company, 1995.

Horan, Nancy. *Loving Frank: A Novel.* (on Frank Lloyd Wright and Mamah Cheney) Ballantine, 2008.

James, William. *The Will to Believe.* Dover Publications, 1956.

Kachuba, John. *Ghosthunters: On the Trail of Mediums, Dowsers, Spirit Seekers and Other Investigators of America's Paranormal World.* New Page, 2007.

Keefe, Rose. *Guns and Roses The Untold Story of Dean O'Banion, Chicago's Big Shot before Al Capone.* Cumberland House Publishing, 2003.

Kennedy, Dolores. *William Heirens: His Day in Court.* Bonus Books, 1991.

Lanctot, Barbara. *A Walk Though Graceland Cemetery.* Chicago Architecture Foundation, 1982.

Larson, Erik. *The Devil and the White City.* Vintage, 2004.

LaVey, Anton S. *The Devil's Notebook.* Feral House, 1992.

Lindberg, Richard. *Return to the Scene of the Crime.* Cumberland House, 1999.

Madsen, Axel. *The Marshall Fields: The Evolution of an American Business Dynasty.* Wiley, 2002.

Malamud, Bernard, and Kevin Baker. *The Natural.* Farrar, Straus and Giroux, 2003

Markus, Scott and Mary Czerwinski. *Voices from the Chicago Grave.* Thunder Bay Press, 2008.

McRae, Donald. *The Last Trials of Clarence Darrow.* William Morrow, 2009.

Miller, Donald S. *City of the Century: The Epic of Chicago and the Making of America.* Simon & Schuster, 1997.

Moore, R. Laurence. *In Search of White Crows: Spirtulaism, Parapsychology and American Culture.* Oxford University Press, 1977.

Morrison, Hugh. *Louis Sullivan: Prophet of Modern Architecture.* Smyth Press, 2007.

Oleszewski, Wes. *Ghost Ships, Gales and Forgotten Tales: True Adventures on the Great Lakes.* Avery Color Studio, 1995.

Possley, Maurice. *The Brown's Chicken Massacre.* William Morrow, 2009.

Pridmore, Jay. *Inventive Genius: The History of the Museum of Science and Industry, Chicago.* Museum, 1996.

Reynolds, Francis. *Lady Elgin: The Lady is Down.* Sarge Publications, 2003.

Russo, Gus. *The Outfit.* Bloomsbury USA, 2003.

Sabina Khan, Yasmin. *Engineering Architecture: The Vision of Fazlur R. Khan.* W.W. Norton & Co., July 2004

Steiger, Brad. *Psychic City: Chicago, Doorway to Another Dimension.* Doubleday & Company, 1976.

Stonehouse, Frederick. *Haunted Lakes: Great Lakes Ghost Stories, Superstitions and Sea Serpents.* Lake Superior Port Cities, 1997.

Sullivan, Terry, and Peter Maiken. *Killer Clown: the John Wayne Gacy Murders.* Pinnacle, 2000.

Theodore, John, and Ira Berkow. *Baseball's Natural: The Story of Eddie Waitkus.* Bison Books, 2006.

Wendt, Lloyd. *Give the Lady What She Wants: The Story of Marshall Field & Company.* And Books, 1997.

Willrich, Michael. *City of Courts: Socializing Justice in Progressive Era Chicago.* Cambridge University Press, 2003.

INDEX

AUTHOR BIOGRAPHY

Photograph courtesy of Ilse Cowan

A recognized authority on the Chicago region's ghostlore, historian, author, and parapsychology enthusiast Ursula Bielski has been writing and speaking about Chicago's supernatural history, folklore, and the paranormal for more than twenty years. Her interests in ghosthunting and local legends began at a young age. She grew up in a haunted house on Chicago's North Side and received an early education in Chicago history from her father, a Chicago police officer. Since that time she has been involved in various investigations of haunted sites in and around Chicago, including such notorious locales as the Country House Restaurant in Clarendon Hills, Illinois; Chicago's Red Lion Pub; southwest-suburban Bachelor's Grove Cemetery; and the Oshkosh, Wisconsin, Opera House.

Bielski and her books have been featured in several television documentaries, including productions by the A&E Network, The History Channel, The Learning Channel, The Travel Channel, and PBS. She appears regularly on Chicago television and radio, and lectures throughout the year at various libraries and to historical and professional societies. She has also authored numerous scholarly articles exploring the links between history and the paranormal, including pieces for the International Journal of Parapsychology. Bielski is a past editor of PA News, the quarterly newsletter of the Parapsychological Association; a past president and board member of the Pi Gamma Chapter of Phi Alpha Theta, the national history honor society; and a member of the Society of Midland Authors.

Bielski graduated from St. Benedict High School in Chicago; Benedictine University in Lisle, where she received a B.A. in history; and from Northeastern Illinois University, where she earned an M.A. in American cultural and intellectual history. Her academic explorations include the spiritualist movement of the nineteenth century and its transformation into psychical research and parapsychology; and the relationship among belief, experience, science, and religion.

In 2004, she founded Chicago Hauntings, Inc., a company that gives bus tours and holds special events devoted to exploring Chicago's haunted history.